D0971197

To:_____ From:_____

Heavenly Patchwork

Quilt Stories Stitched with Love

by Judy Howard

Docas Publishing, Oklahoma City, OK.
www.heavenlypatchwork.com

Unless otherwise stated all Scripture citation is from The MacArthur
Study Bible, Holy Bible, New King James Version, copyright 1979, 1980,
1982 by Thomas Nelson, Inc. Scriptures marked NIV are from the New
International Version.

Although the author and publisher have made every effort to insure the
accuracy and completeness of information contained in this book, we
assume no responsibility for errors, inaccuracies, omissions, or any incon-
sistency herein. Any slights of people, places, or organizations are unin-
tentional.

Second printing 2006

ATTENTION QUILT GUILDS, QUILT SHOPS, CHURCHES,
NON-PROFIT ORGANIZATIONS, COLLEGES, CORPORATIONS,
UNIVERSITIES: Quantity discounts are available on bulk purchases of
this book for fund-raising, educational or gift purposes. Special books or
book excerpts can also be created to fit specific needs. For information,
please contact Dorcas Publishing, 12101 N. MacArthur, Suite 137,
Oklahoma City, OK 73162; ph 405-751-3885, dorcaspublishing@cox.net.

Endorsements for Heavenly Patchwork

"The inspiring stories in this book are sure to warm your heart and soul." *Jinny Beyer, author, fabric designer, teacher, lecturer and winner of 1978 Great American Quilt Contest.*

"Make a quilt — warm a heart. This book, Heavenly Patchwork, proves how a quilt can provide solace in times of need. It makes me proud to be a quilter today." *Georgia Bonesteel. Check out her new release Georgia Bonesteel's Quiltmaking Legacy, www.georgiabonesteel.com*

"This collection of stories bring us the history of everyday women through the memories of each storyteller. Historians of tomorrow will go to books like this for a sense of quilts and quilters of the past." *Judy Anne Johnson Breneman, Quilt History Enthusiast & Writer*

"I'd like to paraphrase a quote from my own book, Quilting To Soothe The Soul, to endorse Judy Howard's wonderful book, Heavenly Patchwork: When there is joy or stress in your life, turn to your needle and let the labor of your hands work through the images in your heart. Judy's book exemplifies all the good feelings of acceptance and resolution quilting brings to the quilt maker and receiver. It is a 'must have' addition to any personal library!" *Linda Carlson, author www.lindacarlsonquilts.com.*

"Written with religious conviction, Heavenly Patchwork conveys the meaning of quilts within the context of giving and receiving via short stories that are fun to read. They recap an event or time when needed comfort was provided by a quilt. For inspiration, these stories are followed by a Biblical quotation. Reading the tales makes me happy to be a quilter." *Patricia L. Cummings, Quilter's Muse Publications*

"It has always been my hope that each and every quilt be a product of the maker's heart as well as her hands. The quilts featured in these stories are special because they were created with love, gifted with love and received with love, continuing the tradition of quiltmaking in the best possible way." *Judy B. Dales, quiltmaker, teacher, author, lecturer www.judydales.com*

"One of the great privileges of working with quilters and being part of the quilting industry is seeing first-hand the compassion that surrounds us collectively. Judy Howard's collection of stories is a beautiful example of heartfelt efforts to provide peace and

support to those most in need. Quilters have a keen ability to comfort and sooth, but also strengthen, always while creating the patchwork that binds us together."
Beth Hayes, Editor McCall's Quilting

"Every quilt tells its own special story and reveals something about the hands that stitched it. This book sets those stories to paper so that all of us can hear the whispered secrets of how quilts are woven into the fabric of our lives." **Melanie Hemry, award-winning writer and winner of the coveted Guideposts Writing Contest, and author of ten books.**

"My grandmother was a quilter, bringing life to new and old remnants of fabric. Like my grandmother's quilts, Heavenly Patchwork weaves stories about life — past and present. This book will warm your heart and lift your spirit."
Louise Tucker Jones, Award-Winning Author and Speaker

"I feel in my heart that each of the quilts that you tell about, each quilt that has been made and given away has a story to tell." **Helen Kelley, author of Every Quilt Tells a Story and Helen Kelley's Joy of Quilting, helenkelley-patchworks.com**

"Curl up with a cup of coffee and read these heart-warming true stories — sure to touch you, lift your spirits, provide a laugh and add joy to your day!" **Jan Krentz - Quilt Teacher, Author, Designer**

"Quilts represent everything good in our lives — love, comfort, generosity, warmth, home, memories, creativity, beauty. Heavenly Patchwork explores the meaning quilts have in the lives of their makers and recipients. Your purchase of this book will bring the comfort of quilts to thousands more through the charitable work of dedicated volunteers who make quilts for children, hospitals, homeless shelters — all the people and places in need of the touch of love quilts represent." **Nancy Kirk www.kirkcollection.com**

"Quilts hold so many stories, if they could only talk. They help get us through the good times and the bad times, and hold those memories for us. I love reading these stories of strength and courage and how fabric helps get us through." **Katie Pasquini Masopust, teacher, lecturer and author of art quilts.**

"A wonderful, uplifting and interesting read for those who love quilting... and God. It's also for those who know neither quilting, or God." **Chalise Miner, writing teacher and author of countless articles and book, Rain Forest Girl.**

"I have known Judy Howard more than six years. Her quilts for charity, prayers and Christian business ethics are very evident. These stories all have a common thread — women sew quilts with a prayer in every stitch that the one who uses the quilt will be well and safe." *Sharon Newman, author of 14 quilt books, teacher, appraiser, lecturer and former owner of The Quilt Shop in Lubbock, Texas.*

"Heavenly Patchwork's heartwarming stories offer a peaceful respite in our busy lives, and celebrate the special roles women have played in our nation's history." *Sarah Orwig, author of 71 published novels with 20 million copies in print.*

"A charming book that is as filled with historical lore and insight as it is with delight. A quilt lover's dream." *Laura Palmer NYC Author of Shrapnel in the Heart and Television Journalist.*

"Quilts chronicle the lives of those who made them and those who have used them through the years. Enfolded within each and every quilt, embraced between the layers, are touching narratives. Ms. Howard has collected some of the best and offers them to us in her wonderful book!" *Susan Talbot-Stanaway, Executive Director, Museum of the American Quilter's Society, Paducah, KY*

"Your wonderful book proves my point — every story in life is a quilt waiting to happen. I enjoyed your nice stories and the idea of sentiments and things that make our hearts feel good. Keep up the good work. I think it is wonderful that you are giving your proceeds to quilting people who share their gift." *Mary Lou Weidman, www.Marylouweidman.com*

"All quilts have a story to tell and what could be better than a collection of these stories? Wrap yourself in your favorite quilt, have a box of chocolates within reach and settle in for a wonder read!" *Janet Jones Worley, teacher, designer and author of Quilts for Chocolate Lovers.*

"What a wonderful, inspiring book and how touching the stories. The world has no idea how much quilters touch the lives of others. Many local organizations are now making quilts that are donated to the military for the returning wounded service people. Other groups are making quilts for the Sharp Hospital Burn Camp for Kids, Cancer Camp for Kids, Children's Hospital, and a host of other organizations in need. We know how much these quilts mean to the recipients, and we know in our hearts how good it makes us feel to be able to create and donate them. *Heavenly Patchwork* tells this story over and over, and is a great source of comfort and inspiration. What a great gift for Mother's Day!" *Betty Alofs, Designer, Teacher, author, Betty A's Designs*

Contents

*Dedicated to quilters everywhere, past and present, who
capture and preserve our history through their quilts.*

Acknowledgments

Creating Heavenly Patchwork has been an exciting challenge made possible and enjoyable by the many companions who have helped along this journey. My heartfelt gratitude and thanks to:

My loving husband, Bill, who encouraged me. Family and friends who faithfully prayed, advised, read and edited the stories: Chalise Miner, Dorothy Palmer Young, Rhonda Richards, Dr. Ann Lacy, Dr. James Alexander, Barbara Shepherd, Maggie Abels, Caleb Smith, Laura Palmer, Frederica Griffith, Jean Stover, Dr. Don and Janet Addison, Bill and JoAnn Jones, Marsha Mueller, Kay Bishop, Louise Tucker Jones, Rick Akers, Jean Stover, and Cheryl Pierson.

Carol Wallace, Shelli Johnson and children, Kay Bishop, Deborah Johnson, Joan Currie, Tracy and Kevin McGehee and children, Jean Stover, Betty Crompton, and Harn Homestead for photo modeling and settings.

Fred Welch, Welch Creative Services, welchcs@swbell.net, who did the layout and graphics and cover photo.

And most importantly to my heavenly Father who prompted me to compile these stories to inspire women to look to Him for their source of joy, strength, comfort and healing; and to everyone who submitted their heart-warming true stories.

We invite you to send your stories for future editions to: HeavenlyPatchwork@cox.net 12101 N. MacArthur, Suite 137, Oklahoma City, OK 73162-1800. Check for writing guidelines at www.heavenlypatchwork.com, and for 300 pictures of antique quilts you can add to your collection at www.buckboardquilts.com.

Preface by Rhonda Richards

Quilters seem to know intuitively how to respond to other's needs. A few years ago I dealt with my own long-term struggle— watching my mother's health decline as she spent a year in the hospital. By God's grace, she recovered and lives independently again. Although her turnaround was a miracle, there were days so dark that I couldn't see hope in anything.

It was during that difficult year that I contacted Judy Howard about featuring her and her work in <u>Great American Quilts.</u> I had published several of her quilts in our magazine over the years. I explained my situation to Judy. During the months when we were exchanging legal and business documents, it always lifted my spirits to see Judy's hand-written notes on the envelope, "Still praying for you and your mom."

Those words are a testament to who Judy is, and what she has accomplished in this book. In <u>Heavenly Patchwork</u>, you'll find heart-warming stories from women who have experienced God's grace through quilting. There is comfort in cloth. Who has not felt soothed when wrapped in a quilt lovingly made just for them? Or how many times have you gotten through a difficult period in your own life by keeping your hands busy stitching?

I love the promise in Revelation 21:4: *"He will wipe away every tear from their eyes. There will be no more death or mourning or crying or pain..."* Until that time, I believe we are to love and comfort one another. And if you are a quilter, God can use that talent to bless others.

The psalmist once asked, *"How can I repay the Lord for all His goodness to me?"* (Psalm 116:12) Christ taught us that when we minister to the needs of others, it is as though we are doing it for Him. Quilting may be your expression of God's love. Let the following stories inspire you with God's message of hope, mercy, comfort and faithfulness to sustain us in our time of need. Rhonda Richards, Editor of the <u>Great American Quilts</u> book series.

Introduction

by Judy Howard

In September, 2003, after 27 years of selling antique quilts in Oklahoma City, I moved my shop home to do web business. For the next seven months of tumultuous adjustment, feeling disconnected and useless without a shop to open, I prayed for God to give me new purpose and direction.

Three days after starting Beth Moore's <u>Believing God</u> Bible study, He revealed his new dream for me — to write a book of quilt stories of how women have pieced their brokenness into beauty by believing God. Using my own intellect and abilities, I knew His dream for me was absurd. But He has proven faithful and all-sufficient to meet my needs, and verified His promise that indeed "All things are possible with God."

The definition for healing is to mend by stitching. God brings wholeness and restoration as He cradles me in His loving hands and joins my broken pieces together, forming a stronger and more beautiful creation to glorify Him. Healing is the process of connecting with the Great Physician and learning to depend on Him.

My prayer for you is that this book will inspire you to seek and find the only true source of comfort, healing, joy, and fulfillment in Jesus alone. May you never grow impatient, discouraged or hopeless in waiting on Him to complete this process of piecing your brokenness into beauty, one stitch at a time.

All book profits go to non-profit organizations that make quilts for the needy. No salaries or expenses other than the actual layout and graphics, printing & shipping costs will be deducted from the total sales to figure the profit. All other expenses of time, labor, photography, advertising and editing are excluded and considered a voluntary contribution toward the cause.

Mail the **ORDER FORM** in the back of this book for additional copies of <u>Heavenly Patchwork</u> for friends and family or for your **Quilt Guild** or **Church Fund-Raising** to benefit children & families in crisis situations. Your support can make a difference. Thank you.

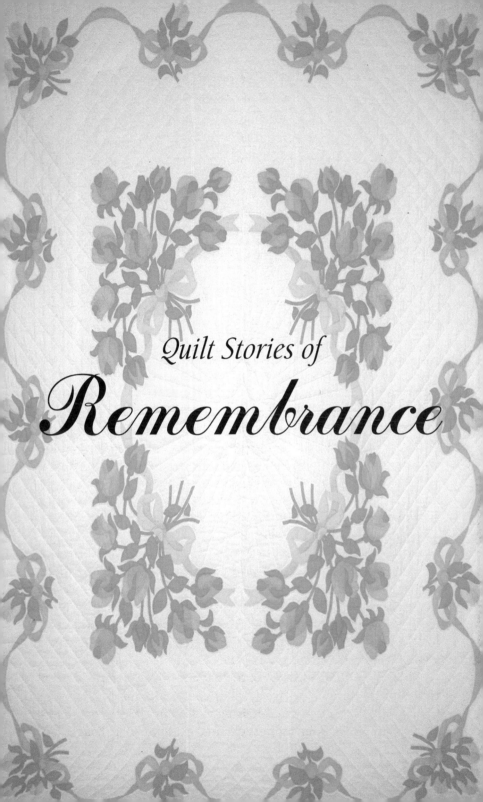

Quilt Stories of
Remembrance

The Living Quilt

by Nancy Harris

Memories blanket the old house like a patchwork quilt. Drawn from the far corners of the country, cousins come to the reunion, sewn together by the common thread of family. It is a long and colorful thread, beginning in Denmark and winding its way to the prairies of Kansas in the late 1800's. From an old land to new they came. The everyday hardships of frontier life honed and strengthened them, each crisis stitching them closer to the land and to each other.

Today, the cousins gather in the house their grandfather built. The house, stone barn, washhouse and silo still stand as silent testaments to the workmanship of bygone days. Sorghum fields, pumpkin vines, horses in the pasture, and old trees meandering along the creek bed give a nostalgic patchwork picture of days and ways long gone.

After lunch, exploration of the house begins in earnest. In the parlor, tatted doilies lend nostalgic elegance to modern tabletops, and heirloom crystal vases hold fresh peonies. Climbing a narrow staircase, the cousins walk through small bedrooms. Carefully folded at the foot of old beds, threadbare quilts with fabric now faded into muted colors get particular attention.

"I remember Grandma always had a project stretched on the frame, ready for quilting whenever she had a free moment. She said it was her evening entertainment."

"Does anyone remember our evening entertainment?" The laugher starts before the story is even told. "We would take turns sitting on a quilt and the older kids would drag us around and around on the wooden floors until Grandma climbed the stairs and put an end to our shenanigans." Smiles cross faces recapturing the days of such simple fun.

"Did you ever wrap up in a quilt and sneak onto the upstairs balcony to stargaze?"

"Yes, and I remember falling off that balcony during a wrestling match," one of the men chimes in.

Suddenly someone spots a familiar piece of material in the

quilt and a particular dress or shirt is brought to mind. There seems to be a story with almost every square. "I don't think Grandma ever threw away a piece of material, always saving for another quilt."

As the quilts are unfolded, and life stories reveal the love sewn into each quilt, it becomes obvious that Grandma never meant for them to be showpieces, but made them to be "comforters".

Later in the afternoon the very same quilts are tossed on the grass and the kinfolk sit in the shade of an old tree. They thumb through yellow, brittle-paged photo albums where the somber faces of their ancestors stare back. Stiffly posed, dressed in black and clearly uncomfortable with the presence of a camera, the subjects in the photos do not smile, but instead impose their dignity for posterity.

Looking at the photos it is easy to see that the vestige of familiar facial features... the eyes, a chin or nose... are not just history but alive in this generation. Like the material reused in a patchwork quilt, so the family lineage continues to pass from generation to generation.

"Look, look at Great Grandpa's chin... all the men in the family still have that little clef."

"Well, unfortunately this survived the gene pool," and several giggle as they cover their protruding ears.

The afternoon passes in fond remembrances. As the cousins tell their own stories, the living quilt grows ever more colorful, varied and complex. So it is, piece-by-piece, story-by-story, year-by-year, the quilting continues. Comforted by the knowledge they are stitched together forever by the thread of family, they wrap themselves within their quilt of legacy and love and say their good-byes.

> *"I thank my God upon every remembrance of you, always in every prayer of mine making request for you all with joy,"*
> *Philippians 1:3*

A Quilt for Chase and Colton

as told by Kathy Wilburn Sanders

Kathy Wilburn woke with a slow stretch before remembering the date. April 19. Years before on this date she'd given birth to her daughter, Edye. She rolled over and smiled into her pillow. Edye was a grown woman and mother now, and that umbilical connection from mother to child had stretched to include a whole new generation — her sons, Colton and Chase. Kathy glanced at the clock, and pulled herself out of bed to dress for work. She and Edye worked in the same building in downtown Oklahoma City. Kathy couldn't help but wonder how Edye was feeling this morning. She'd been home with strep throat the past two days, but her co-workers had baked a cake and planned a surprise party at the office. Edye knew something was up and wouldn't want to miss it.

Just as Kathy suspected, Edye dropped Chase and Colton off at the daycare located in the Alfred P. Murrah Building before reporting for work. "Surprise! Happy birthday!" Candles stood on the birthday cake like sentinels with blazing hats. Laughing, Edye took a deep breath and blew...

At that moment, a rental truck loaded with ammonium nitrate blew half the nine-story Murrah building into oblivion. Candles wobbled as the building where Edye and Kathy worked trembled from the blast.

Kathy could hear panic clawing at Edye's throat. "Mom, what if it hit the boys?" They raced through smoke, debris and falling glass to the Murrah Building. The blast that felled the Murrah Building on April 19, 1995, left a crater in the hearts of Kathy Wilburn and Edye Smith. Two-year-old Colton and three-year-old Chase both died as a result of the bombing.

For nearly two weeks, the whole world watched as exhausted rescue workers pulled bodies from the rubble. After the smoke cleared, 168 people were dead and 400 injured in the worst terrorist attack to date on U.S. soil. The whole nation mourned with the families of those slain.

For the next six years, Kathy traveled the country trying to weave together the events leading up to that fateful day. She retraced the paths Timothy McVeigh and Terry Nichols took leading up to the bombing. She explored white supremist and anti-government groups. Her investigative reports were used in the documentary, "A Cry for Justice: The Untold Story Behind the Oklahoma City Bombing," produced by MGA Films and released after Timothy McVeigh's execution in April, 2001.

Chase and Colton's family never got to say goodbye. They weren't even allowed to view their bodies. Kathy clings to the chipmunk underwear Chase wore that morning. "I've kept their clothes and toys as reminders, because that's all I have left of the boys," Kathy says. "On April 19, 1995, their lives were erased, and we were left with lives we didn't choose.

"My husband was furious with God, and died of pancreatic cancer two years after the bombing. I didn't know why the boys died, but I knew I couldn't get through the pain without God's grace, which proved sufficient. I now know that God didn't take my grandchildren, but received them when they died."

Many people responded with acts of kindness, but one stands out to Kathy Wilburn. Susan Smart, from Enid, Oklahoma, called and asked for photos of Colton and Chase. Six months later, Kathy's doorbell rang and Susan presented her with a beautiful quilt covered with all the boys' pictures, telling the story of their lives.

Another memorial quilt featured a little boy with angel wings in the center, surrounded by Nine Patch blocks and star quilting on a cloud print background. The penned inscription reads, "In memory of Colton and Chase Smith, Budded on earth to bloom in heaven. A gift of loving stitches from Lincoln Quilter's Guild."

"I carry the scars from that day just as if I were burned," Kathy says. "But I've learned that every day is a gift from God that I must spend wisely." April 19, 1995, is one such day. It's the day of Chase and Colton's death. It's also the day their mother was born years earlier.

Sometimes the loss seems to outweigh the joy. When that happens, Kathy wraps herself in a quilt and the joyous memories it holds.

> *"My grace is sufficient for you, for My strength
> is made perfect in weakness."*
> *2 Corinthians 12:9*

Belief in Tomorrow
by Shirley J. Bergman

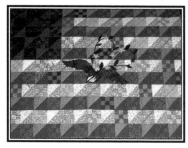

"We have just received word that a plane has hit one of the World Trade towers." For days I watched the TV news as the tragedy unfolded. *I have to do something,* I thought. *Something to bring some order to all the chaos.*

As a long-time quilter, I pulled out all the red, white, and blue material from my fabric collection. Events of the days that followed directed my emerging American Flag quilt. I covered my machine quilting lines with gold and silver feather stitches, done by hand. Next I hand embroidered the first line of "America, the Beautiful". I then appliquéd the eagle, soaring with a heart-shaped olive branch, dotted with leaves and stars, symbolizing our yearning for peace. God Bless America, the enduring American spirit and my profound respect for the many heroes of those horrific days, led me to title my quilt, "To Comfort and Honor".

Quilters from throughout the world were called to action by the Quilt Heritage Foundation, challenged to show "our hope and belief in tomorrow — the American spirit will triumph over tragedy." Twelve quilts, with their stories, were chosen for the American Spirit Quilt Collection to tour the United States.

Since our quilt group planned to have a quilt show Labor Day week-end for the town's annual Peach Festival, we investigated the possibility of adding the American Spirit Quilts to our show. We held fund-raisers to bring the Collection to St. John Lutheran Church, Romeo, Michigan.

The 12 beautiful quilts arrived, and our three-day show opened. Over 600 people came to see the traveling 9-11 quilt exhibit, as well as the 125 community quilts we had draped over the pews. Docents pointed out the details and sentiments stitched into the memorial quilts: "Over 3,000 different fabrics were used in this quilt... Then 700 images of the missing were downloaded from the CNN website by quilter Lois Jarvis, and used in the star for the making of 'Ground Zero'... A class of third graders made the next quilt. Their teacher, Jane Dodge, created this quilt called 'Prophecy of Peace'... Coming all the way from the Republic of Singapore... The verses of a hymn are printed and appliquéd onto the crazy quilt, 'Freedom is Not Free'... 'For God and Country' is dedicated to Fr. Michael and the firefighters who knelt before him receiving absolution..." and it went on.

Hung from the balcony facing those American Spirit Quilts, an eagle of peace with olive branch clutched in its beak, soared across the red and white stripes of a quilt. It rose above our nation's tragedy with hope and belief in tomorrow, a gift of comfort to all in soft cloth — this quilter's triumph over tragedy.

> *"Now thanks be to God who always leads us in triumph in Christ . . ." 2 Corinthians 2:14*

Piercing Memento of Quilting Bee

by Anita Burger

"For Pete's sake. I'm sick and tired of ripping out all these big stitches the minister's wife took last week. You know Mrs. Alexander is such a perfectionist she'll never be pleased with this workmanship. If she weren't paying us 50¢ a spool to quilt her daughter's wedding quilt, I'd leave these stitches in."

"Hush your complaining. Here comes the preacher. Don't you let on what you're doing. His wife would never speak to us again if she knew. When is your husband going to Chicago again? We need a supply of those small fine needles he found last year. You can't make decent stitches with these toad stabbers we're using now."

"Bessie, honey child, come out from playing under the quilt and thread our needles for us. My eyes aren't what they used to be, and this dim light doesn't help any."

"Do you think we can finish this quilt today if all eight of us stay til five? I'd sure like to put in my grandbaby's crib quilt next week. You know Millie's due any minute! I'll come back tomorrow morning if we don't get finished tonight. Can anyone join me?"

Such was the conversation around the quilting frame of the Ladies' Aid Society at their weekly quilting bee in the First United Methodist Church Fellowship Hall in Coweta, Oklahoma, in the early 1930's. They brought their sack lunches to share and quilted from 9:00 a.m. until 4:00 p.m. while their preschoolers played happily under the canopy of the quilt. When the summer temperatures got too hot in the church, they moved their quilting frame outside under the shade of the huge oak tree.

"Did you hear about Louise's daughter eloping with the butcher's son last week? Louise is heartbroken! She had always dreamed of giving her only daughter a fairytale wedding — the one she never got for herself. And pray for Bessie's gallbladder operation. As much chocolate as she eats, it's no wonder she's having trouble. Do you think we should take turns babysitting for her six little ones and taking meals over?"

Before anyone could reply, they all jumped in unison when they heard a blood-curdling scream from under the frames. "What on earth is wrong with you Anita?" her apprehensive mother questioned. With tears streaming down her face, two-year-old Anita emerged holding her knee up for a kiss. "She must have been crawling around and got a needle in her knee. I'd better take her to Dr. Gentry to try to dig it out before it gets infected."

Dr. Gentry performed exploratory surgery the next day on little Anita, but never found the needle. It wasn't until Anita had her knee replaced 60 years later that the surgeon spied the illusive needle on an x-ray.

"Every time I look at my needle surgery scar, I think about the fun times the ladies spent together quilting, visiting, and sharing all the intimacies of their personal lives, both good and bad," Anita related. "The intimate fellowship around the quilting frame was the only reason Mother joined the Ladies' Aid Society."

My Mother, one of nine girls, grew up on a large farm. The girls took turns working in the fields with the hired hands. She would trade with a sister so she wouldn't have to do housework. Mom hated housework, cooking and needlework. But since volunteering was a way of life in her family, she always delighted in helping the needy through the church quilting. Whenever there was a tornado, flood or a fire, The Ladies' Aid Society dropped what they were doing to supply warm blankets and food for the victims. They could tie four dozen heavy, wool comforters in one day if all 12 of them helped. They truly exemplified the Golden Rule.

"In everything I did, I showed you that by this kind of hard work we must help the weak,..." Acts 20:35a NIV

God Still Multiplies Loaves and Fishes

by Judy Howard

"We must be out of our minds to get up early on a freezing Saturday to stand in line, outside in 30 mile-an-hour northerly winds for 30 minutes with hundreds of other idiots," I grumbled to my friend, Mikie Metcalfe, huddled next to me.

"I wish I were back home in my nice warm bed with this cup of coffee," Mikie said. Then she went on chattering to warm herself and take our minds off our freezing toes. "Clara Rosenthal Weitzenhoffer's estate sale had better be worth this cruel and unusual punishment. Did you know her house just sold for a cool $2.5 million? And they're saying now that the art collection she gave to the University of Oklahoma is worth more like $200 million rather than the $50 million they originally thought."

"No kidding. Where do you suppose they got all their money?" I asked rubbing my hands together.

"Her daddy was a wealthy oilman in Kansas and she married an even wealthier oil man. They built this huge mansion on five acres in Nichols Hills with one wing just for her Mother," someone standing nearby volunteered.

"But why would they donate all the furnishings to the University of Oklahoma along with the art? Didn't they have children?" someone asked.

"They only had one son, Max, who won two Tony Awards as the Broadway and London producer of Will Rogers Follies. He operated an art gallery in New York City and currently is Head of the Drama School at O.U. I think they're going to build a gallery in order to recreate room settings of the mansion with the original furnishings for the art," a man behind us answered.

"Can you believe no one in Oklahoma even knew all that priceless art was right under our noses? Mr. Weitzenhoffer died ten years ago and Clara refused to spend the night in their mansion again. Caretakers have been maintaining the estate and grounds ever since," the classy lady in front of us said. "I've lived right down the block from them all these years and had no clue. We've always admired the Dalmatian statues flanking their front driveway but never once saw anyone coming or going."

When the policewoman finally called my name, I elbowed my way through the throngs of people into a tiny room containing more than a dozen quilts, linen, lace and textiles.

I prayed for wisdom, guidance and keen eyes to make "yes, no or maybe" decisions to purchase on the spot. Since 9/11, the antique quilt business was pitiful, along with the rest of the economy, and my bank account was barely out of the red. In that mob scene, just stretching out each quilt to examine it was a major struggle, as well as protecting it from being snatched from my arms by other interested parties.

After an hour of exhausting deliberation, I hauled six quilts to the front register and left bids on five others that were stained or not quite as desirable. I pumped the people in charge, as I always do, for the family information. I was delighted to learn that Clara Rosenthal along with her mother and grandmother probably made the quilts themselves in the late1920's.

After reexamining the quilts at the shop and reconsidering the value of their provenance of historical significance, I became more comfortable in justifying my large outlay of cash.

Several years earlier, after studying Jesus' miracle of multi-plying the loaves and fishes to feed 5,000, I had been convicted to give back to God to multiply the best quilts He brought to me. Therefore, I decided to give 100% of the proceeds of Clara's quilt sales to God to multiply to feed and shelter the homeless at Grace Rescue Mission in Oklahoma City.

Several hours later, I was shocked to receive word that my bid for the remaining five quilts had been accepted. This was a miracle in itself considering the swarms of interested buyers at the sale. It had to be a "God thing." He had saved those quilts for me to be used somehow in His Kingdom.

Because the responsibility of pricing Clara's quilts was too overwhelming for me, I asked the national quilt appraisal guru, Sharon Newman in Lubbock, Texas, to appraise them. I was shocked to find the collection was worth $20,000 because of the family's philanthropic leadership in Oklahoma.

I asked God for wisdom to market and advertise the collection. He led me to call Daily Oklahoma writer, Marcia Shottenkirk.

She came out immediately with a photographer, and her article appeared in the next Saturday's Religion section. I also mailed flyers to all my customers.

Four days after the initial offering of the quilts, God sent one of my favorite customers to the shop to buy four of the 11 quilts to raise $9,000 for Grace Rescue Mission. I immediately mailed the $9000 check to the homeless shelter and drug and alcohol rehabilitation center. Then I waited with joyful anticipation for God to act again. I knew He would.

Within one month, I was able to mail another $4,000 in checks from sales to Grace Rescue just in time to meet their greatest winter needs. I mailed another $4200 check two years later from Clara's quilt sales, and donated the remaining items directly.

What a faith-builder to witness first hand God performing again His miracle of multiplying my meager resources offered to Him in faith. I've never experienced greater joy than when God sees fit to use me in His work. It causes me to weep with thanksgiving just remembering His goodness.

> *"And Jesus took the loaves, and when He had given thanks He distributed them to the disciples, and the disciples to those sitting down;... So when they were filled, He said to His disciples, 'Gather up the fragments that remain, so that nothing is lost.'"*
> *John 6:11-12*

Jean's Last Quilt

by Kay Steiger

Stepping into Jean's world was more like stepping into the antebellum south than into the hospice of a terminally ill cancer patient. A true southern belle and an antique dealer, Jean surrounded herself with elegance and feminine niceties like her dainty rose teacup collection, chintz floral china, and elaborate silver dresser sets. Her home wafted with the scent of tiny fragrant floral soaps. She had a knack for bringing the outdoors in, and her happy surroundings meandered outside her window to the birds feeding on her sunflowers.

My relationship with Jean began as a good deed for her, but quickly became a gift I gave myself. While I planted her favorite flowers, Jean shared her cooking secrets, charming social graces, and marvelous stories spoken in her enchanting southern drawl.

As weeks turned into months, I made the startling discovery that Jean had become closer to me than my mother, sisters or friends. She taught me the value of the precious Present — how to savor each moment as a celebration of life.

While her spirit soared, I saw cancer ravage her body and knew that Jean's approaching birthday would be her last on earth. I wanted to give her the perfect gift, something to give her both comfort and joy in her last days. What could it be? We were kindred spirits, I reminded myself, so what would I want?

I instantly knew the answer. It was the quilt I'd coveted for my own 1850's half-tester plantation bed. It was a reproduction "Baltimore Album" with intricately appliqued rose wreaths, birds, butterflies, bridal bouquets, cornucopias overflowing with flowers, undulating bud and vine borders, inner sawtooth borders and embroidered with "Sweet Flowers Bright as Indian Sky."

As Jean's world became more confined to the bed, the quilt would bring flowers and all the beauty of the genteel south to surround her there. When she opened my gift and saw the quilt, tears streamed down her face. "This is the most beautiful quilt I've ever seen," she said. "Even when it's dark at night and

I can't sleep because of the pain, I can trace the outline of these flowers and birds and be cheered."

After sharing my faith with her and praying with her many times, I asked Jean specifically what we should pray for her. When she said, "Accepting," I thought she meant accepting the reality of her situation. When it became evident later that she meant accepting Christ as her savior, I panicked and felt totally inadequate.

I held her frail hand in mine atop the "Baltimore Album" quilt and told her about Jesus' love and forgiveness. Tracing the flowers of that quilt, we discussed how we can be victorious over death because Jesus rose from the grave. Jean's fear of death turned to praise as we sang hymns. Jean had time to share her faith with her family before she went to her Bridegroom's wedding feast and mansion in heaven. She experienced for herself that Jesus did indeed remove the sting of death in His resurrection.

It's been ten years since Jean left us with all those tender memories. I visited her husband weekly until his death a year later. Occasionally I see her daughter and granddaughter who still cherish Jean's "Baltimore Album" quilt as a reminder of her genteel ways and passion for the beauty of God's creation.

Knowing how much both Jean and that quilt meant to me, my husband bought me an identical one for my birthday. It adorns our antique bed and is a constant reminder of the love and good times Jean and I shared. I'm looking at it as I write, and I thank God for giving me the great privilege of knowing Jean and introducing her to the Creator, the Comforter and Prince of Peace.

"Death is swallowed up in victory. O Death, where is your sting?" 1 Corinthians 15:54-55

The Fabric of Our Lives
by Jeanne Dunlap Knol

My life has been interwoven into the fabric of quilts. When I was 17 months old my mother placed me in my big wicker buggy and tucked me safely into the quilt my grandmother had pieced. Papa removed the buggy's wheels and carefully positioned the buggy into the back of our Model-T Ford. Then off the family rumbled on my first long journey from San Francisco to Grandma's home in western Oklahoma.

During those "Depression Days" we often journeyed to Grandma's. At night we crawled into bed, sank deeply into a billowy feather mattress, and covered ourselves with quilts Grandma had affectionately constructed from various family members' cast-off woolen coats and trousers. The pot-bellied stove in the dining room provided meager heat to counteract the howling winds and blowing snow. But those quilts, so heavy I could barely turn over, supplied a fiber-fuel that warmed not only the bones but radiated deep into the soul.

Living in the middle of the Dust Bowl, I vividly remember Grandma digging out every quilt she could find to cover the windows and doors. The quilts became homemade ventilation filters that created a safety net to protect us from the grime-ridden gusts and the wailing winds.

In the mid-30's, Papa worked in the oil fields. It was common to move to Oklahoma, Texas, Illinois and Louisiana four or five times a year. Each time, we packed everything we owned tightly into one car, including the Singer sewing machine turned upside down on the floor of our Model-A. This left just enough room at the top for a comfy pallet of quilts to cushion my dog and me. As we traveled along looking out at the world, I often thought, *Pug and I have the best seat on the road.*

When my mother passed away, the family quilts came to me: the Dutch Doll pieced from scraps of my dresses, the Four-Patch made by Grandpa, the California Star, the String quilt, the velvet and silk Crazy, the Flower Garden, and so many more.

But the most treasured of all is the one Grandma pieced from Bull Durham tobacco sacks. After a hard day's work, late at night by the light of the coal-oil lamp, she ripped apart each sack. Gingerly she washed the pieces, then dyed them with herbs from the garden, ironed them, and finally pieced everything into a quilt. Although it is faded now and certainly not the loveliest, my youth is restored each time I see it. My spirit soars as I am reminded of the countless blessings and sacred memories woven deeply into Grandma's quilts. Oh, that each of us could have this joyful fiber sown into our lives!

> *"The LORD is my shepherd;... He restores*
> *my soul;" Psalm 23:1-3*

A Treasured Heritage

by Velda Brotherton

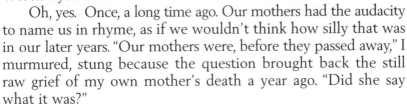

I leaned back to enjoy having my hair washed, scarcely listening to the beautician's words,. . . "and she said that going through her mother's things, she found something she wanted you to have."

"I'm sorry, who?"

"Nelda. Her mother died last month. Weren't you friends?"

Oh, yes. Once, a long time ago. Our mothers had the audacity to name us in rhyme, as if we wouldn't think how silly that was in our later years. "Our mothers were, before they passed away," I murmured, stung because the question brought back the still raw grief of my own mother's death a year ago. "Did she say what it was?"

"No,. only that she'd tried to reach you a few times. Maybe you ought to give her a call." She stripped water from my hair, and I sat up so she could pat it dry.

A few days later I called Nelda, who still lived in the town where I had once spent a brief time with my great-grandparents before the world I knew as a child came apart. Moving back to Arkansas after all those years, had been my attempt to put the pieces of my life back together. "Nelda, this is Velda," I said when she answered.

Laughing, she replied, "Hi Velda, this is Nelda." We still thought our mothers had been besotted, but really they'd only been very young and happy to have carried and birthed healthy daughters with the world in such turmoil. Still, our rhyming names continued to amuse us. "Glad you called," she went on after a moment. "I have something . . . In Momma's things I found a quilt. Pinned to it was a note. Can you stop by the next time you're in town? I think you'll want to see this."

"I have a checkup at the clinic next Wednesday. I can stop by after if you'll be home."

She said she would and maybe we could have coffee and visit a while. She wouldn't tell me about the note, wanted me to see it for myself. I thought maybe she was having a hard time talking about it, her mother's death being so recent, so I didn't press her.

My mother's passing had been the hardest time of my life. Grief continued to strike me at the most unexpected moments. This was one of those times, and when I hung up the phone I began to cry. I still hadn't found the strength to face her loss and be happy with my life like she would have wanted me to. We were so close, and I'd made the mistake so many do of never imagining there would come a time when she would be gone. Gone forever. Sadly, most of us never think of what that means until it becomes a reality. Stuck somewhere between guilt and acceptance, I struggled to restructure my life, without much success.

I drove the familiar scenic highway through the Boston Mountains of the Ozarks, its curves and steep inclines capturing most of my attention. The trees were turning from shades of green to the burnished reds and golds of autumn and the air smelled of wood smoke. I found Nelda raking leaves in the back yard, and she greeted me as if glad to be done with the chore for a while. Though we hadn't grown up together, the bond we had because of our mother's friendship assured we were at ease with one another. We chatted about our families, where the kids and grandkids were and what they were doing while she put on the coffee and set out cups, spoons, sugar and cream.

It wasn't until she poured the coffee and sat down that she brought up the quilt. Her fingers patted at a slip of paper lying on the pristine white tablecloth as she talked. I noticed her hands were wrinkled and old and glanced at mine. Odd, we were supposed to still be young, and here we sat, looking like our mothers, who had gone on to their rewards.

She held the paper a while longer, staring at it through eyes that gleamed with unshed tears, then handed it to me, her hand trembling. "Momma wrote this. I found it pinned to an old quilt. It looks like not too long before she . . . uh, see how the letters are a little shaky?"

Joined together in grief as we had once been in friendship, we gazed at each other for a silent moment before I took the note. Tears blurred the writing, and I batted my eyes several times, then glanced at the spidery letters that formed the short note. It read: "Give this to Velda. It was her great-grandmother

Smith's, and I know she'd like to have it." The kitchen was so quiet we could hear the ticking of the clock above the refrigerator. "She must have given it to Momma," Nelda said, and cleared her throat. Then she took a folded, well-worn patchwork quilt from a chair scooted under the table where I hadn't seen it. "All those years ago. So long ago." Tears ran unashamedly down her cheeks and I wiped my own.

Then she held it out to me, one hand supporting the precious bundle, the other covering the top. I took it with the same reverence. I felt as if she were giving me back a grandmother I'd all but forgotten, a memory held in trust and returned when I most needed it. And in passing on the quilt that day she gave me something else as well: the ability to cherish the gift of my own mother's love, to realize the way all mothers are bound together, one after the other in an unending chain. That kind of love never dies, but is carried down through the generations. This gift I will gladly pass on to my daughter and hope one day she understands the value of it.

In 1941 we moved from our rural home to live with my great-grandparents so I could start to school. I was five. Though many are convinced they remember back to the beginning of their lives, I only recall my great-grandmother through photographs. This tiny woman, dressed in a long black skirt, a loose black sweater and cloche hat worn low on her forehead, stirs only the vaguest of memories. Caught forever as solemn and unsmiling, she stares from those blurry black and white photos as if wondering who I am. Perhaps she would not recognize me today. My mother told me she was a cheerful, kind woman, and that Grandpa put up with having two small children invade his quiet home with silent dignity.

When the war broke out, my parents, brother and I moved away from Arkansas, and Grandma and Grandpa Smith returned to their home in Kentucky. I never saw them again—until the day Nelda handed me that quilt and visions of Mother, Grandmother, and Great Grandmother all coalesced and became a treasured heritage.

Great-Grandmother's quilt hangs today in the living room on a quilt rack alongside a top pieced by Grandmother, and a Friendship quilt pieced and quilted by Mother and her friends when I was a baby. Though I will always miss my mother, I no longer grieve her passing. Instead I thank God for the years we had together and for all those whose love has made this life so rich and fulfilling.

> "May your unfailing love be my comfort,"
> Psalm 119:76 NIV

State Fair Brings Bonanza
by Judy Howard

"Boss, there's a rough looking character here who says he wants to pay for new tires for all his carnival trucks in quarters. What do I do?" asked the flabbergasted tire shop manager trying to conceal his laughter.

"Tell him sure thing. We'll be happy to mount them for him. Ask him to have the bank president roll the quarters for him first so you don't have to count them." Then with a chuckle, he added, "That's old Joe Coopersville."

Each September when the Oklahoma State Fair comes to town, all the shop owners in close proximity to the fairgrounds seek solace from each other, swap bizarre incidents and bemoan sagging sales. One of my favorite annual customers runs the Midway Ferris wheel rides. She pours out her tales of woe as well as high intrigue about life on the carnival circuit. It's fun to help her pick out tiny quilts to brighten up her travel trailer.

Such was the case in September of 1994. A flamboyant lady in sexy clothes and heavy make-up pushed her way through the Buckboard Antique Quilt shop door behind a heavy box of blankets that she wanted to sell. As we spread out each quilt, she spilled out the heartaches, hardships and also the exciting stories of adventure on the road as a "Carnie." She was the Magician's Assistant — the woman they stuck swords through in the box.

Though the six handmade scrap-bag quilts she had made on the road between gigs were crude, she succeeded in expressing her inner beauty in this art form. Out of compassion, I bought the quilts. After all, an interesting provenance is said to add $100 value to a quilt. Never had this proved truer. Though the quilts were not valuable, the person behind the quilts was priceless — especially in God's *eyes*. This fascinating lady's life story sold her quilts.

The Image

by Martha Baxley

My grandmother was typical of her time, only more so. Besides bifocals and the long gray hair pulled back into a bun, she wore long dresses. I thought she looked exactly like the picture on the Old Dutch Cleanser can.

She was never still and considered wasting time one of the Seven Deadly Sins. Beside the usual household duties, she raised a big garden and canned her own food, had large flocks of chickens, guineas, and turkeys and managed a small herd of cattle. Some of these were milked twice daily, the milk run through a cream separator and the cream sold once a week. She rose daily at four a.m. to start her daily routine.

I marveled that the tiny woman, only five feet tall, could cover so much territory. As she scurried diligently from chore to chore she seldom spoke, but wore a pleased little smile, as though her accomplished tasks gave her inner peace. Even when she sat, she worked. There was always a basket of peas to shell, a pan of peaches to peel, mending or sewing or the everlasting quilts needed attention. If none of these tasks was urgent, she read the weekly *Kansas City Star* or the *Farmer-Stockman magazine,* which was all she could afford.

"My grandmother saved all the scraps of cloth from her sewing projects and frugally pieced them into quilts. Her quilts were masterpieces of art, worked into intricate patterns: Wedding Ring, Flower Garden, Drunkard's Path, Windmill, Oddfellow.

There was always a quilt in the frame, which hung suspended from the ceiling of the dining room. When it wasn't being worked on, the suspending ropes were wound around the frame's ends to keep it above our heads and out of the way. If no other duties were pending, the quilt was "let down". Then she and anyone else who had time spent the afternoon quilting tirelessly. Time flew as fast as their needles while they married off and buried half the family.

When I was small, I supposed that my grandmother had always been old, gray and wore bifocals. I never wondered that her name was Martha, just like mine, or that she seemed to try to live up to the true Biblical meaning of it.

When I was a newlywed, I was given a portrait of my grand-parents taken on their wedding day. Imagine my shock when I saw behind her bifocals eyes suddenly familiar in a hauntingly familiar face — a carbon copy of myself.

> "Martha, Martha, you are worried and troubled about many things. But one thing is needed, and Mary has chosen that good part . . ." Luke 10:41 NKJ

Civil War - Hidden in Plain View

as told by Oma Dolores Campbell

My grandmother, Oma Johnson was my hero — a great storyteller and a quilter. I loved to sit at her feet as she was quilting to hear her tell about her grandmother Etta Mae who grew up during the Civil War.

"Tell me the story about the Yankee soldiers marching through the countryside torching and ransacking all the farms," Dolores pleaded.

"Well, the day I'm thinking about," Grandma Oma would begin, "Etta Mae and her mother had just taken her eggs and milk to town to trade for a special bolt of calico fabric to make Etta Mae's wedding quilt for her dowry chest. As the Yankee soldiers approached, Etta Mae panicked and flung her prized bolt of fabric behind the outhouse out of desperation to protect it. After spending the afternoon in the dark, musty root cellar with the spiders and mice, her dad gave the all-clear signal and Etta Mae and her mother came out praising God for sparing them and their home. Only a few chickens and only half the tomatoes had been confiscated.

"Etta Mae raced out to retrieve her fabric and was shocked to discover that, somehow, it had unrolled all the way down the hill — decorating the war-worn hillside for everyone's enjoyment. All the neighbors had a good laugh about Etta Mae's landscaping beautification program as they gathered the next Sunday in church. They had much to rejoice about in God's hand of protection and in His sense of humor," concluded Grandma Oma.

> "He shall cover you with His feathers, And under His wings you shall take refuge;" Psalm 91:4

K9 Heroes of Murrah Building Bombing

by Cindy Todd

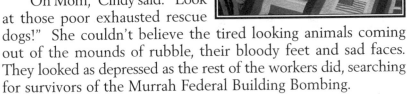

"Oh Mom," Cindy said. "Look at those poor exhausted rescue dogs!" She couldn't believe the tired looking animals coming out of the mounds of rubble, their bloody feet and sad faces. They looked as depressed as the rest of the workers did, searching for survivors of the Murrah Federal Building Bombing.

"My heart breaks for this whole thing, but especially those dogs!" agreed Arlene. "Something about their valiant efforts. I wish there was some way we could pay tribute to their heroic work." Almost immediately, Arlene Todd reached for her sewing basket, suggesting, "We should make a quilt to commemorate their part in the rescue efforts."

"Fabulous idea, Mom," Cindy agreed. "You can design and quilt it. If you need help, Artie and I can pitch in." Already moving toward the idea, Cindy suggested, "We can gather colored pictures of all 38 search and rescue dogs and transfer them onto white quilt blocks, two to a block."

The two collected the pictures from the Oklahoma Pet Hall of Fame and Quantum Trading Cards in Edmond. Arlene came up with the clever idea of bordering the blocks in the symbolic colors of the ribbons worn by Oklahomans during their work: purple for courage, blue for statehood, yellow for hope, and white for innocence.

Both Cindy and Arlene always believed the quilt was divinely inspired. For instance, Arlene picked the chain pattern for the quilting simply because she liked it. But it took on more significance as the chain link fence became the temporary memorial at the bombsite and was later incorporated into the finished memorial. They kept making mistakes in their rush to finish. The errors on the quilt showed them that God has a sense of humor and wanted the quilt to bring smiles.

"You see," Cindy explained, "we accidentally included one dog twice. Ironically that dog's name is Ditto."

As one of the rescue workers wrote to Arlene after seeing the quilt, "With all our diverse ethnic, religious, and cultural differences, a hundred thousand Tim McVeighs couldn't tear us apart. He only made us Oklahomans come closer together." He added, "It's people like you who show the world that we as a nation will survive. . . we will heal. . . we will stand together. . . we will rebuild. . . and we will never forget."

The Rescue Dog quilt captures the essence of my mother," Cindy said, "her love of God, her desire to help others and her Oklahoma Spirit."

Arlene Todd went home to be with the Lord last year. The quilt has become Cindy's most reassuring possession — perpetually honoring Arlene as well as the K-9 heroes.

"Behold, how good and how pleasant it is for brethren to dwell together in unity!" Psalm 133:1

The Centennial Quilt

by Holly A. Doyle

At age 31 I was absorbed in sewing classes. I failed 8th grade sewing since I never completed my blue skirt with the giant yellow ducks on it. I am sure I selected the fabric just to get on my Mother's nerves and to say "See, I can't sew." Yet here I was, decades later, attending a two-hour sewing class. I was making my own pants, vests, tops, and accessories as well as gifts for my family and friends. I could whip together a vest in less than an hour.

The American Sewing Guild, which I attended, met in a sewing shop in Pennsauken, New Jersey. One evening a representative from the township came to speak to the group. They wanted a quilt made to celebrate the 100 years of Pennsauken's history, but all attempts to find a group willing to help had failed. They asked us to help out. I considered myself a sew-er and not a quilter, but the others in the group thought it would be a great project to take on and eagerly volunteered. They nominated me to coordinate, organize and delegate tasks

I met some great quilters who stood right beside me and whispered advice in my ear. Things were happening quickly so I listened eagerly. After much discussion the themes were selected. I learned that Jersey Joe Walcott came from Pennsauken; that red fabric will run, and blue fabric will come off on your hands. I still have scraps of those fabrics in my stash to remind me of these lessons.

There were people involved in the project who did not sew at all. Some used glue to attach their design and other had photographs transferred onto the fabric. Some spent hours and hours making exquisite blocks. I created an Apache Indian, complete with a beaded headdress, to mark my years in the marching band and a bowtie block in honor of Mr. Phifer, an icon in the Pennsauken school system who was never seen not wearing a bowtie. I also made a replica of my church. These blocks alone were great accomplishments for me, but they didn't prepare me for the parade.

In May of 1992 the Township of Pennsauken held a huge parade to celebrate the centennial. Bands, fire trucks and hundreds of people showed up for this big event. The plan was for the quilters to ride on a float with the quilt. When the float finally arrived, imagine our surprise to discover it to be a pirate ship! There was room for only a handful of quilters, but no room at all for the quilt. So we draped it off the back of the ship. The rest of us walked — or rather ran — behind. Our pirate ship was going at quite a clip.

As we marched I could hear the ooh's and aah's of the crowds as the quilt passed by where they stood. As we approached the announcer's booth, we could hear the puzzlement in his voice, but then the excitement as he saw the long awaited quilt which commemorated this landmark occasion. It was then that it hit me. I had been a part in bringing together a diverse group of women to create a meaningful keepsake of our town's history.

Although the gifts I brought to the project were not quilting, I had other God-given gifts. After all, a gift is not a gift if you keep it for yourself. I had shared mine with others. I was happy, proud, a bit sad and relieved all at the same time. Someone had seen my gift and gotten me involved. Assembling the quilt was a huge undertaking, but the joy that it gave me to see the end result still awes me. I still think of the words of wisdom and encouragement that were passed to me each step of the way. Surely God had brought this all together!

The Pennsauken Centennial Quilt is now permanently hung in the W. Leslie Rogers Library on Route 130 South in Pennsauken. God sent messengers to show me the way. The courage, compassion and strength came entirely from Him. The quilt revealed·God's plan for my life and He continues to show me ways in which I can use my sewing and quilting skills to bring joy, inspiration, and comfort to others. Now I am the teacher and pray for my students that they will also experience the joy found in doing God's work with a needle and thread.

> *"There are different kinds of gifts, but the same spirit."* I Corinthians 12:4(NIV)

A Tribute to Dad
by Alice Kellogg

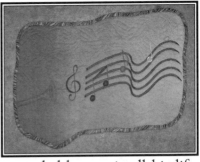

Although my dad, Ralph Doughty, was a self-taught musician, he had a God-given talent that he loved to share. He was born on a farm near Fairview, Oklahoma, in 1920, and was surrounded by music all his life. His father played the fiddle, his mother played the piano, and all seven of his siblings played an instrument. As a boy he branched out from family hoe-downs to playing his trumpet on street corners for anyone who'd listen.

During WWII, Dad played in the army band and also fought in the Battle of the Bulge. After the war, he married and went back to college to complete his MBA, dedicating his thesis to me. Dad enjoyed a career as Budget Forecaster for Kerr-McGee, but his first love was music. He played on his lunch hour and on weekends. He arranged music and performed in the company talent shows, even doing gigs in nursing homes.

While Dad surrounded my nights with music, my days in high school home economics were a sour note for me. I hated that class, but I did eventually learn the basics of sewing. Dad's mother gave me some Sunbonnet Sues that she cut from dress scraps. Mom taught me how to embroider all the little decorative stitches on the bonnets and shoes. She showed me how to use a long running stitch to applique the pieces onto the blocks. Then I gave them back to Grandma who set the blocks together and sent them to the Mennonite women in Fairview to hand quilt. The finished quilt was a scrapbook of treasured memories from childhood, which I love to this day. Meanwhile, Dad celebrated life with music.

In 1967 Dad wrote a Jazz Mass for St. Patrick's Catholic Church for Thanksgiving. The following year he arranged a jazz version of the Lord's Prayer which he played at my wedding. He told me how proud he was of me while he walked me down the aisle.

Every eye in the ballroom was riveted on me and my groom as we took the floor for the first waltz at our wedding reception. Other couples soon danced to the beat of Al Jenning's Dixieland

Band in which Dad played. My husband was readily adopted into the family band that performed at every family gathering. They called themselves the Cimarron River Rats, because they had to cross the Cimarron River to get to the family reunions in Fairview.

When Dad died in 2001, I decided to memorialize his life in a quilt as a lasting tribute to his musical talent. A quilting class with Trish Stuart inspired me to use her technique of painting images on fabric with crayola and inks that look like applique. Using that technique, I painted Dad's beloved trumpet with a treble clef and staff blasting out of the bell of the horn. The first black quarter notes signify that he lived a long full life... but life is short. The second note is blue and short symbolizing his short illness. The white note is death. A longer half note travels toward the gold whole note, symbolizing his final reward in heaven. The background color graduates from a dark to a light blue as if going toward the light.

I hand quilted it with angel wings fluttering above the staff. The musical symbols quilted in the lower third are shadows of music falling off the staff. I copied the quilting design on the bell of the horn from the engraving on his trumpet.

My husband cried when I finished Dad's quilt. Though it hasn't won any ribbons or awards, it is priceless to me for the memories it evokes and the loving tribute it pays to my dad, whose musical genius brought gaiety and enjoyments to thousands.

I miss you Dad!

> "... the trumpeters and singers were as one, to make one sound to be heard in praising and thanking the LORD,"
> 2 Chronicles 5:13

A Century of Quilts

as told by 101 year old Maude Chenoweth Leaman

Christmas on the Farm

The day dawned cool and crisp. Eight-year-old Maude Chenoweth could hardly wait to help Papa cut down a Christmas tree. She had already been making paper ring garlands and popcorn chains to trim it. It was Christmas Eve and excitement was everywhere.

"Come on Papa, let's get the horse and wagon and go out into the field to cut our Christmas tree," Maude prodded as she jumped up and down in excitement.

Papa quickly harnessed the horse. Maude and her older brother Earl jumped in the wagon just as snowflakes started falling. "This is going to be the best Christmas ever," Earl exclaimed as they cut down and loaded the biggest cedar tree they could find.

Little Maude was Mama's extra right hand — helping in the vegetable garden, feeding pigs, milking cows, churning butter, making bread, and sewing. After they set the tree up outside the front door and decorated it, Maude hurriedly started mixing and kneading the dough for the 12 loaves of bread she helped Mama make each week. After all the chores and cleaning up after dinner, she stayed up late cutting paper dolls out of a catalog, backing them with cardboard, and dressing them in scraps of calico from the dresses and quilts she and Mama had made.

"I'm making dolls for all the mothers and girls, and hemming feedsack handkerchiefs for all the men and boys," Maude explained as her mother started to send her to bed. "Please let me stay up until I'm finished. I want to surprise all my aunts and uncles and cousins with a gift when they come tomorrow." Exhausted as she finished the last gift, Maude fell into a sound sleep.

The next morning, Maude raced from her bed to discover what Santa had left in her stocking. She tore open the wrappings and found a beautiful doll — her first real doll. She hugged her mama and papa with tears running down her cheek and exclaimed, "She's beautiful!"

Papa carefully hung the exquisite doll out of harm's way on the wall behind the pot-bellied stove. Maude dutifully helped Mama with the morning chores.

As Earl had predicted, the Christmas of 1912 was the best one ever. When the rest of the family arrived, a filling Christmas dinner was served. Everyone loved their handmade paper dolls and hankies. The cousins built snowmen as the adults inspected the two-story addition to their little two-room house. Then they all gathered inside to hear the Bible story of Jesus in the manger. They sang carols while Mama played the old pump organ. What a celebration to remember!

Two days later, Maude began to sew clothes and a tiny quilt for her prized doll. In horror, she discovered the face was running down and all deformed. To everyone's surprise, the doll was made of wax and had gotten a little too close to that pot-bellied stove.

Maude cried herself to sleep that night as Mama rocked her. Little Maude never forgot what Mama told her that night, "When life gives you scraps, make a quilt." Maude was learning early in life to look for the good in every circumstance.

Marriage Frontier Style

Eighteen-year-old Maude nervously stood, dressed in her Grandmother Chenoweth's white lace and pearl wedding gown. Mama piled her long hair on top of her head to pin the veil in place. Maude suddenly burst into tears, "Mama, I'm scared to death. Were you this jittery on your wedding day?"

Mama assured Maude that her jitters were normal. "You will be fine when you see Clarence, you'll see!"

Neighbors and family had gathered from nearby farms. They brought quilts and other gifts to help the new couple set up housekeeping. The traveling minister performed the ceremony in the beautiful flowering garden of their two-story clapboard farmhouse. After a buffet lunch, cake and punch, the guests bid the newly married couple farewell as they took off in her father's Model A Ford with tin cans clanging.

The young couple stayed busy. Clarence worked a variety of jobs; Maude continued to help her mama and papa with the chores and responsibilities of raising her nine younger siblings as much as she could. Clarence and Maude began a family of their own with the birth of a son.

When the Great Depression hit and Clarence lost his job, Maude encouraged him to set up his own electrician's shop. Maude worked 12-hour days beside her husband as bookkeeper, receptionist, store manager, and eventually mother to three rambunctious boys.

Every night after tucking their boys into bed, she pulled out her needle and thread and her sewing machine. She made their clothing and new quilt tops to cover their old tattered and well-worn quilts to keep them warm. She milked a cow every morning before work, and paid her neighbor with milk to quilt her tops. Life without daughters and working full-time at the shop meant that Maude had to raise a garden and do all the domestic chores without help and with little money to waste on store-bought items.

Whenever she started feeling sorry for herself, Maude would pick up her piecing and quilting to chase away the gloomies. She gave herself a good talking-to, suggesting she change her attitude. It was during these lean years, that Maude was forced to trust in the Lord to supply all their needs and renew her strength.

Economic times were hard. Clarence moved his little family to Oklahoma City in search of a better life. Maude took in washing and ironing, babysitting and sewing for a dollar a day, and found a job as an alterations seamstress to pay the mortgage on a little house they bought in 1943.

Over the years, Maude and Clarence provided a home for many members of their extended family. Their generosity took many forms. Maude never forgot working all day, coming home to fix dinner and cleaning up for eight people, then quilting until 2 a.m. They always had a quilting frame set up in the living room for Mama to quilt on during the day. The only problem was that Mama could only quilt in one direction, so Maude had to stay up late to quilt from the opposite direction so Mama could continue quilting the next day.

Maude's hands were never idle, but always helping someone — quilting, and crocheting or sewing doll clothes. She was convinced her heavenly Father was in control and never doubted

His everlasting love. But it was her quilting that calmed her down and enabled her to change her focus from self-pity to praising God again.

God Sustains Maude through Tragedy and Loss

During the 1960s, Maude suffered a series of major losses. Her widowed mother was the first. A few years later, she said good-by to her beloved Clarence. That same year, Maude was devastated when she received news that her oldest son Gordon had been killed in a plane crash.

The pain she experienced seemed unbearable. "Though my family and church were tremendously comforting and supportive, it was only the healing balm of God's love that sustained me as I repeatedly gave Him my grief. There was a hole in my heart the size of the Grand Canyon. The Lord eventually gave me a pinhole of light in my dark valley. He led me through the sorrow and restored my strength and joy. I never blamed God for my heartaches. I know God is good. It is Satan who comes to kill and destroy.

"When I occasionally feel down, I ask Jesus to show me some way to extend His light of love to others by sharing His loving kindness to those even needier than I am. During those dark times, I've also turned to piecing and quilting and dressing my dolls for consolation. It's helpful to get my mind off myself and create beauty to share with others.

"I've also lost five brothers and sisters, but God has always been faithful to comfort and heal my broken heart and bind up all the wounds as He rocks me, wrapped in His quilt of love."

Maude the Torch Bearer at Age 98

On a hot, sunny day in 2002, Maude walked down to the end of the block to watch the cross-country Summer Olympic Torchbearers hand off their torches to the next partners in the historic relay. Children jumped up and down with excitement as they screamed out, "They're coming, they're coming."

They stopped right in front of Maude for the historic picture -taking ceremony. The young torchbearer shocked everyone by handing the lit torch to Maude instead of his partner. After asking her age, the runner gave Maude a big sweaty bear hug and an Olympic flag to add to her collection of firsts.

Maude has always been a torchbearer, reflecting the light of Jesus' love and giving sacrificially of herself through service and quilts. Since 1922, she's made over 100 quilts and given almost every one away to appreciative family, friends and neighbors. She's gifted 200 patchwork pillows and bags to mastectomy patients. Each stitch of each beautiful quilt is a labor of love and creativity — a legacy of a woman of great faith who has poured out her life as a drink offering to God in service to others.

Since Maude retired from her full-time job as seamstress at the age of 74 in 1978, she's kicking up her heels and enjoying the time of her life. She joined a doll club and made a Friendship quilt signed by each member that was featured in a doll book. Her drawers overflow with blue ribbons for her dolls and quilts; and her scrapbooks bulge with pictures and stories of all the quilts she's created.

One of her favorites is the Butterfly quilt fashioned from blocks she embroidered and painted with crayons in the 1930's, which she finished after retiring. Then there's the blue and white Burgoyne Surrounded quilt Maude made from scraps from Kerr's department store uniforms. She won a blue ribbon for her Drunkard's Path quilt.

People were always giving Maude quilt blocks to finish. One time the St. Luke's Church choir director found some State Flower blocks in his Mom's estate. There were three state blocks missing, so he searched the Internet and presented Maude with the missing state blocks for Christmas. Since he was retiring, she finished the quilt and gave it to him as a going-away present.

"My current passion is making my Fun quilts or I Spy quilts which I laid awake one night fashioning in my mind," Maude enthusiastically explained. "I love to personalize them. I've made one with different sports cars in each block for my grandson, and toys and teddy bears for baby quilts, and roses for the women. I surprised my granddaughter with a quilt at her wedding shower. She and her mom both burst into tears of joy. That's what makes it all worth the time and effort," Maude added, a little bleary-eyed herself.

Maude's Centennial Celebration

It's February 5, 2004, a day after Maude's 100th Birthday Bash.

I'm exhausted. There must have been well over 100 people here, Maude mused. *I'm worn out from all the festivities and the crowds. I need something to calm me down.*

Maude did what she always does when she needs to relax. She took out the bright, cheery pictorial blocks she had cut for her Fun quilt and began piecing them together.

As she fed the fabric through the sewing machine, her mind went back to the Christmas in 1910 when Papa surprised Mama with a shiny new-fangled treadle sewing machine. He had built up credit for months at the general store in town by bringing in eggs, corn, cream and a butchered cow. "Now Cora and Maude can stitch our clothes, bedding and mattresses much faster than by hand." her father had explained.

Maude was the oldest girl and Mama's extra right hand, always by her side helping with everything. After her younger sister was born, Mama's doctor prohibited her from using that treadle sewing machine because of the phlebitis in her legs. This presented a big problem since Maude was too small at six years old to even reach the pedal to take over the sewing. Papa came up with the perfect solution. Mama could instruct and supervise. Maude could stand on her tiptoes and guide the material through the machine. And Earl, her older brother, could squat down and work the treadle with his hands. Talk about family togetherness!

United they conquered the chore, and bonded in the process.

Sewing and quilts had played a major role in Maude's family even before she was born. Maude's great grandmother, Mary McElwain Chenoweth, appliquéd a red and green Eagle quilt top in 1860 for her son who fought in the Civil  War. It was a family heirloom which traveled in a covered wagon in 1889 to Hinton, Oklahoma. Maude's mother and her two sisters-in-law quilted the top in 1900 and inscribed in the quilting "Presented to Benjamin Franklin Chenoweth by his mother 1860."

Quilts seem to have always formed the backdrop for her fulfilling Oklahoma life. Maude never forgot that icy cold water as the Methodist minister from Hinton baptized her in the stream in the canyon when she was 12. Mama dried her off and bundled her up in a warm quilt until she quit shivering. Afterwards, the little church family celebrated with a picnic spread out on quilts as the children frolicked and played in the lush meadow.

For years, Maude's mother entered quilts in the Oklahoma State Fair. Maude, too, had many blue ribbons to her credit. It would be impossible to count the number of quilts Maude had made for her children, grandchildren, and great grandchildren over the years. Even nieces and nephews were blessed. When Maude's sister-in-law, Mildred Chenoweth, set out to create a Grandmother's Fan legacy quilt for her own granddaughter, Kristin Chenoweth, Maude contributed the perfect pink ruffle for the border of the project.

Now, as Maude guided her new blocks through her sewing machine, she felt calm and recharged. That first treadle sewing machine was only the beginning of a lifetime of stitching in love for her family.

"What is your secret for a successful life?" Maude was recently asked.

"Life has given me lots of pieces of sorrow and hard work, but I always was determined to keep on smiling through the tears, and loving and helping as Jesus did," Maude replied. "Like my Mama always said, 'When life gives you scraps, make quilts!'"

That's a pretty good recipe for success.

"Rejoice in the Lord always...Be anxious for nothing, but in everything by prayer and supplication, with thanksgiving, let your requests be made known to God; and the peace of God, which surpasses all understanding, will guard your hearts and minds through Christ Jesus." Philippians 4:4,6

Signed, Sealed & Delivered

as told by Clair Schuler's grandchildren

Eighty-seven year old Clair Schuler's grandchildren were going through her old trunk in preparation for moving her to a retirement center. When they asked her about the blanket with all the names on it, Clair explained that it was her brother Walter's baby quilt the ladies at the church made in 1928 when they heard her mother, Edna, was expecting. They enlisted Clair to mail squares of calico to everyone on their Christmas card list. So Clair wrote a note asking everyone to embroider their names and addresses on the squares so they could surprise Edna with an envelope quilt.

When the women completed the quilt, they showed it to Clair before wrapping it up for the baby shower. "Do you think she'll like it?" they asked.

"Oh, she'll love it. But where are the stamps for the envelopes?" Clair asked.

"We hadn't even thought of that. You're right. That would be the perfect finishing touch. But there's no way we could get it done by tomorrow night. If you want the stamps Clair, you'll have to appliqué them on yourself since it was your idea."

Clair worked feverishly all night and the next day cutting and appliquéing stamps onto each envelope.

At the shower, tears ran down Edna's cheeks as she opened the box and examined each familiar name. "It's beautiful! It makes me feel so special and loved. Thanks to each of you who worked so hard on it. But where did you get all these names and addresses? And where did you get the idea for the stamps for the envelopes?"

"Clair collected all the signed squares, and the stamps were her doing as well," one of the women explained. "We think it was a stroke of genius, and certainly has our stamp of approval. Now Walter has his own quilt — all signed, sealed, stamped and delivered."

> *"...you were sealed with the Holy Spirit of promise..."*
> *Ephesians 1:13-14*

Precious as Gold a Spool of Thread

as told by Leora Simpson

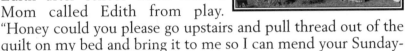

In 1930, 12-year-old Leora Simpson was visiting her friend Edith after school when Edith's Mom called Edith from play. "Honey could you please go upstairs and pull thread out of the quilt on my bed and bring it to me so I can mend your Sunday-go-to-meeting dress."

"But Mrs. Simpson, your quilt is so beautiful. Surely there's another way. I'd give anything for a penny to buy a spool of thread for you, but I haven't laid hands on a penny in months. It breaks my heart to see you sacrifice that wonderful quilt, thread by thread, to stitch Edith's dress."

"Thank you Leora for having such a warm and sensitive heart. I'm glad you appreciate the time and love that went into the wedding quilt my Mother made for me. But it's my only choice," Edith's Mom lamented with tears in her eyes.

Leora had helped her own mom make many a thick quilt to keep the family warm during those cold winter nights. She knew how much love and time were stitched into each comforter.

Leora giggled as she recalled the "Blizzard Quilt" she and her husband patched together years later in their oilfield lease house nine miles north of Great Bend, Kansas. "The colder it got, the bigger the pieces for that quilt became," she said. Snowdrifts were 12 to 14 feet deep that winter, and we ran the old gas heater so high it scorched the floor, almost catching the place on fire.

"That's when you have to depend on God to provide for everything, including food," Leora explained. "With water in short supply, we couldn't grow a vegetable garden. After church each Sunday, we'd pack a picnic basket and take that Blizzard Quilt along to sit on down at the creek." The family would fish all afternoon and just enjoy a great family time of laughter and bonding.

"We didn't even know we were poor, because God was always there taking care of us," Leora said with still a bit of wonder in her voice.

Journey of a Lifetime
by Lucille Lacy

It was Christmas of 1938. With my new doll and buggy and one box of clothes, Mama and I waited to board a bus in Lake Dallas, Texas. We would start a new life in Oklahoma City after my parents' divorce. I was sad to leave everything I'd ever known, my seven grown brothers and sisters and our little two-bedroom house, but my good-bye tears soon were replaced by the jubilant excitement of adventure.

With only a $500 inheritance from her parents, less the price of bus tickets, Mama was not quite so jubilant. She would need to find work to support herself and her seven-year-old daughter in the middle of the Great Depression. Mama worked as housekeeper, practical nurse, cook, seamstress and babysitter. We may have been poor, but we were rich in God's blessings in a home full of love.

Three years later, Mama invested the remaining $325 of her inheritance in a two-room home in Calumet, Oklahoma. The house had no plumbing, but did have a good cistern. It was my chore to keep the enamel water and wash tub filled and ready to heat on the kerosene stove for cooking, laundry and bathing. Washday meant continuous trips to empty and re-fill our only washtub and sore muscles from using the rub-board. When I hung the clothes on the line in the winter, they often froze as fast as I pinned them up.

I was Mama's shadow and quickly learned to do everything she did.

Without a car, we walked to Sunday school and church each Sunday. We both made our commitments to Christ and were baptized together. It was faith in a loving God who provided for all our needs that held us together as a joyful little family.

Mama's quilting frames were a permanent fixture in our combination bedroom-sitting room. The frames could be raised up near the ceiling so we could sit or sleep in our shared bed. Periodically, Mama and I had a ball at the local feed store rearranging feed sacks to pick the best calicos for our next quilt or dress. Mama's quilts always won First and Second Place Ribbons at the County Fairs.

From the time I was two years old, Mama saved all the scraps from my homemade dresses. She made a beautiful Sunbonnet Sue quilt with embroidered names of all my playmates on the skirts and presented it to me as my wedding gift in 1950.

God blessed me by giving me this beautiful, Christian mother who cared for me and truly sacrificially loved me.

Mama's life was filled with tragedy. She was only 12 when her own mother became ill. Mama was forced to quit school to run the household, quilt, and raise her siblings. Her own daughter died of diphtheria at age four, and her 24-year-old son died from war injuries. Then her marriage fell apart.

It was during the quiet times spent quilting and piecing that God comforted, strengthened and healed her broken heart. Her quilting gave her a sense of joy, restored her sanity and strength, and gave her a feeling of being blessed as she created beauty from the scraps life had given her. I know many prayers went up to God while she was quilting.

Born in 1900, Mama journeyed on to her real and lasting home in 1967. Mama's courage, strength and love will live on forever in the legacy quilts she lovingly crafted. They are solid reminders of who she was and what she stood for, and they also encourage me when I'm going through rough times.

"Be strong and of good courage; do not be afraid, nor be dismayed, for the LORD your God is with you wherever you go." Joshua 1:9

Quilt Stories of

Healing
&
Comfort

The Lady Star

by Lynne Herbert

Several years ago, my mother gave me an old LeMoyne Star quilt top sewn by an unknown lady. Vibrant diamond shapes of various sizes wobbled their way past puckered mauve sashings, without one point meeting where it should. "How can I possibly finish you?" I asked the haphazard half-done quilt, taking it out frequently to admire the old fabrics and soft muslin.

Thirty years slipped by. One day, feeling courageous, I took the lopsided work apart with my seam ripper, then washed and pressed the pieces carefully. I called my project The Reprieved Star. As I worked to salvage it, I felt a gentle rapport with the lady who had attempted to make the quilt. After drafting a new pattern and piecing together the 20 blocks by hand, I was dismayed to find that each block was only 9 1/2" square, far too small for a bed-sized quilt. Back it went into the UFO cupboard.

The following year, I became seriously ill and was hospitalized with heart failure. "Listen to your body," my doctor warned me. My body told me to rest. Still I had to do something. I needed to quilt. I studied the Reprieved Star blocks once again, and decided I could arrange them on point with alternating muslin squares. I used the mauve sashing to make an outside border to retain the integrity of the lady's hard work, her initial effort and her wonderful color palette.

As God nurtured me, my strength grew. I quilted in the ditch around each diamond and repeated the simple pattern in the plain blocks. My needle seemed to glide through the layers of fabric. I thanked God for the inner peace my project brought, because I knew this was one of His smaller miracles in progress. *How many times have the threads of His design come together in coincidence over the years*, I began to ask myself?

When the work was finished, I renamed the quilt The Lady Star for the lady who had originally sewn it. Each night, as I slept under the lovely coverlet, my health continued to improve. In the end, the quilt and I shared a lot. We were both reprieved.

When my daughter's marriage disintegrated, she brought her

wedding quilt home and tucked it into the back of a closet. "Mom," she asked, "May I borrow your Lady Star? I need a quilt in which to cuddle, and it's my favorite!" Now this unknown lady's star quilt, with all its tender stitching, is helping my daughter to grow stronger and regain her confidence again. Doubtless, God has other plans for such a special quilt, too.

> *"being confident of this very thing, that He who has begun a good work in you will complete it . . ."*
> *Philippians 1:6*

Blankie Bliss

by Lisa Alexander

I groggily answer the late-night phone call.

"Mommy," my eight-year-old daughter Emmali whispers. "Mommy, I forgot my blanket."

She is spending the night, four houses away. I suggest her friend will let her borrow one.

"No, Mommy. She doesn't have anything I can go to sleep with. I need my blankie..."

The blankie! That piece of frayed cloth Emmali carries to bed each night. It was originally part of a nursery set my mother had made, a small quilt with glorious pastel pink and blue angels soaring across flannel skies. Now, the faded seraphim barely cling to the quilt's cotton backing. As a baby, Emmali had loved pressing the soft material against her cherub cheeks and twisting the lacy border between her tiny fingers.

As she outgrew diapers and bottles, I began easing the threadbare blankie from her grasp. She reluctantly allowed me to put it up for safekeeping with her older brother's blankets. All three of the blankets remained tucked away in the top of the linen closet for several years. Then, in a day of spring-cleaning, every towel, sheet, and blanket was removed from the closet. Emmali, then seven, spied a corner of her blankie in the pile and quickly grabbed it, pulling it close to her face as she had done when she was a baby. Since reuniting with this long-ago friend, she has nestled with it each night.

Except on this night, when she phones at nearly 11:00 p.m., begging me to bring it to her. No, she says, she cannot make it through just this one night without it. A former blankie-toting child myself, I understand her desperation.

I plod down the stairs in search of my shoes.

"Where ya goin', Mom?" my 14-year-old son, Riles, asks.

When I tell him about the phone call, he offers to take the blankie to his sister. I smile, remembering the farm blankie he had been so attached to when he was young. He would understand.

On this late night, Riles gets on his bike, flinging Emmali's blankie over his shoulder. As he zooms down the street, the tattered quilt seems to transform into the cape of a super-hero.

Before returning to bed, I stop by my baby's room to hear the reassuring rhythm of her breathing. Grace tugs at her tiny quilt as if she is trying to catch the pastel pink, purple and blue butterflies that flutter across it. Butterflies of beauty they are tonight, though faded they will surely be in years to come.

Faded, but well-loved.

"He gives them security, and they rely on it;" Job 24:23

My Security Blanket
by Ruth Eager Moran

Lights flashed and sirens blared in the cool pre-dawn morning. Ambulance attendants swiftly loaded my gasping husband onto the gurney for the tortuous trip to the hospital. I begged to go along, but was waved away. The EMTs insisted they needed the room to begin the necessary procedures.

I quickly dressed and called the children. I told them their dad had awakened clutching his chest and struggling to breathe, so I called 911. They promised to join me as soon as possible. I then called my neighbors, who volunteered to drive me to the hospital and sit with me until my family arrived.

What a nightmare! The attending doctor met us in the Emergency Room. He announced that my beloved husband, John, had experienced cardiac arrest and was pronounced dead on arrival. I would have fainted if I hadn't been sitting down. I immediately dissolved into a pool of tears. This just couldn't be happening! It surely was all a dream that would soon pass.

As the reality of the situation began to sink in, I sank into a deep darkness. Long, lonely hours stretched endlessly ahead of me as I sat staring at John's empty leather chair. One morning, as I was searching for some records in a closet, my hand touched the familiar softness of an old much-used and abused blue American Eagle bicentennial quilt I had bought for my son's bed a decade earlier. I gingerly pulled it down and draped it over John's empty chair and snuggled into its beckoning folds. This now became my favorite place to sit, curled up in the warmth of the mended quilt. I felt comforted and loved by two familiar objects that worked together as my healing place.

It's been 17 years since I lost John. The pain is still as real today as it was that first morning, but God is healing my broken heart with the help of my security blanket. It's as if God's arms are wrapping me in that quilt, holding me and rocking me as the pain subsides. He replaces the pain with His love, peace, hope, and the strength to face the trials of each new day.

My tattered and torn quilt has seen me through illnesses, surgeries, and sleepless nights. I have spent many nights sleeping in John's leather chair wrapped up in my Eagle appliquéd quilt. Often, when I'm restless and unable to sleep, I'll sink into the awaiting warmth and comfort of my security blanket and find God's presence always there to comfort and cheer me.

My old bicentennial quilt has become a very good and faithful friend — going through good and bad times with me. You see, both of us are survivors. Although the blanket has become my "Security Blanket," I know that my real security is not in that comforting quilt. My real security is in God's unfailing love and His promises that He has made me a super-overcomer, a conqueror, and victorious in all things in Him. The King of Kings and Creator of all has promised never to leave me, nor forsake me. Now that's real security!

> "'I will never leave you nor forsake you.' So we may boldly say: 'The LORD is my helper; I will not fear. What can man do to me?'" Hebrews 13:5-6

Faith in a Brown Bag

by T. Dawn Richard

Eight-year-old Genny assessed me with big brown eyes. A look of mild curiosity flitted over her face, and then she whirled around and ran to join her younger brother, Jesse, on the swings.

"She likes you," Glenn said, lacing his fingers through mine.

"How can you tell? She didn't say a word."

"That's Genny. She's the quiet one. Jesse, on the other hand, will tell you exactly how he feels."

I took a nervous breath. "Are we doing the right thing?" With two children of my own, I faced the daunting task of doubling the number of children in my family with one promise of commitment.

Glenn squeezed my hand. "Don't worry. We'll just take it a day at a time."

This had not been in my life's plan — to divorce and remarry. I had lived through the grief of separation, loneliness, and humiliation, and had even questioned my faith as a Christian. And so had the man I met two years into my life as a single parent.

As we discussed marriage, Glenn and I agreed that we wanted our children to understand the value of commitment, unconditional love and forgiveness. I wavered constantly on those last points.

And so I began a new routine. Each night, I asked God to show me how to be a good mother to these four precious children. I asked Him to help me teach my sons and daughters what it meant to trust Him, despite all of the unpredictable events that would undoubtedly fall upon them as they matured.

Seven years went by, and as that summer approached, I began to look for things for our family to do during Genny's and Jesse's yearly visit. Wandering into a fabric store to browse, I found myself signing up the three "women" in our family for a quilting class! What had I done? I wasn't a seamstress, but I wondered if maybe, with a little instruction, I could accomplish a very simple quilt.

A few days later, the girls and I attended our first class. We would be making something called "A paper bag quilt".

"Just pick out 25 types of fabric each," our instructor told us. "Whatever you choose is fine. It's up to you!"

The girls weren't intimidated. My daughter, Summer, chose a feminine pink-and-flowery scheme, while Genny selected a green-and-gold safari combination. I went with my favorites, Christmas colors and patterns.

Once home, we followed the instructions: Cut the fabrics into strips and place them in a brown bag. Pull the strips out without giving thought to color, pattern or order. Whatever you pull from the bag is what you sew to the following strip. After sewing the strips, they would go back into the bag to be pulled out again haphazardly.

We cut and sewed for four weeks. Sometimes we made mistakes, ripped out seams, and started over. At other times, we held up our quilts in progress and commented. Our work was far from perfect. There were flaws, if you looked closely. The edges didn't always match, and occasionally, we wondered if we were making a mess of things. The dining room turned into a profusion of colors, thread, and busy hands.

At the end of those four weeks of putting together pieces of fabric that didn't look like they would match, thinking the toil and frustration would end up as a huge waste of a summer, we were finished.

Glenn, Calin and Jesse came into the house, and my husband quickly found the camera, ordering us to pose.

As we held up our quilts for pictures, Genny with her green-and-gold safari prints, Summer with her pink girlie one, and me with my Christmas patterns, I thought how closely these quilts resembled our family. We had started with so many different pieces of cloth, some of them torn and frayed, some of them seemingly out of place, some with flaws... and we had sewn our family together, one fragment at a time.

God restored my faith that day. Even with our imperfections, and different expectations, amid frustrations and failed attempts, His work would end in something whole, beautiful and perfect. We just needed courage enough to dip into the brown bag and accept what was there, even when we were tempted to toss it back.

I took the camera from my husband. My daughters wore

huge smiles, their faces flushed with the pride of what they had accomplished. As I zoomed in, filling the lens with their quilts, I caught my breath. I had never seen anything more magnificent.

Covered by the Almighty
by Regina Yoder

"Oh, Mom, this Garden View quilt is awesome," Terry and Melanie said as they hugged me. "It's so warm and cuddly made with flannel."

"Lots of prayers and love covered you and your children as I quilted it," I said beaming. "It was such a joy to piece and fun to quilt, I've decided to make one just like it in flowered flannel."

Unfortunately my quilt turned out to be a disaster! I had to rip it apart and start from scratch with a new pattern. God taught me a valuable lesson. I often try to imitate those I admire. Because of my wrong decisions, He has to rip, cut, sew, make smaller pieces, trim and be creative to salvage the mess I've made. I was reminded of Philippians 1:6, "... He who hath begun a good work in you will complete it... " Praise the Lord, there's hope. He's still working on me and won't give up when I fail.

If my life turns out as loveable, warm and beautiful as Terry and Melanie's Christmas quilt, God and I will both be pleased.

Jill's Wedding Quilt

as told by Lois Pickering

Susie and her mom were anxiously pacing the kitchen floor when the phone rang with the bad news. "Susie, I'm so sorry. The tests on your biopsy were positive and it doesn't look good. We need to schedule you for surgery first thing Monday morning to remove the lump in your breast and see how extensive the cancer is," her doctor reported.

"Oh Mom, what am I going to do?" Susie asked, as she put down the receiver. "Jill and Ryan need me. Bill is working ten hours a day, six days a week in his new job, and traveling every week. How could they survive if something happened to me?"

"Don't let your fears run wild! Everything's going to be all right," Mom tried to reassure her. "You're going to take this one day at a time, trusting God to give you courage and strength each step of the way."

Susie and her mom stood and held each other for a long time. Mom finally broke the silence.

"I know... let's start a quilt for Jill's hope chest. It will take your mind off your troubles."

"But Mom, neither of us has ever made a quilt before. I wouldn't know where to begin. I do need a diversion, though. Maybe my friend Lois could show me what to do."

So Lois and Susie went to the quilt shop. They selected fabrics and a pattern for a variation of the traditional Wedding Ring quilt for Jill's dowry. Together they spent hours laughing and reminiscing about their own weddings as they cut the pieces and started piecing each block by hand. It was a joyful and hopeful time, well spent between surgery, doctor's visits, chemotherapy, and, finally, radiation.

With each good report, they celebrated. But even when there were setbacks, Lois and Susie met to talk and piece. It was a time of bonding, intimacy and sweet fellowship. There was also a sense of urgency to complete their chosen project.

When Bill's company transferred him from Oklahoma to Alabama, Susie was crushed! How would she cope without her closest friend to encourage and support her? How could she ever find the strength and motivation to finish Jill's wedding quilt without her help?

Lois promised to pray and email her daily. She would be her long distance confidant and instructor. "You can call me anytime and we can work through any problem with the quilt together. You know I'll always be here to help you."

Three years passed — precious years in which Susie watched her children grow. Susie persevered through treatments, successes, and setbacks. With deep satisfaction, she finally completed the wedding quilt while laying in a hospital bed. Quickly a friend gift-wrapped and rushed it off in the nick of time for Jill's bridal shower. Susie was too weak to go.

Although Susie went to be with the Lord a week after the wedding, Jill feels her Mom's presence every time she touches that beautiful quilt. She is comforted as she remembers all the love sewn into it, stitch by individual stitch.

> "Now may our Lord...who has loved us and given us everlasting consolation and good hope by grace, comfort your hearts and establish you in every good word and work." 2 Thessalonians 2:16

A Quilted Hug
by Teresa C. Vratil

For most of my mother's life, her idea of sewing was to use scotch tape to repair a fallen hem or a stapler to fix a ripped seam. That all changed when she turned 60 years old and was diagnosed with cancer. The doctors told her she had about six months to live; with chemotherapy, perhaps a little longer.

Mom elected to try chemotherapy, and began a series of long, tedious sessions, sitting in a chair, waiting for the chemicals to drip into her bloodstream.

During this time, she began to work on small needlework projects. That Christmas, all seven of her children received 4 inch by 4 inch framed pictures of geese, chickens, or little hearts. Each time Mom started a project, she told herself she would stay alive long enough to finish it.

Mom's six months stretched to a year. The doctors were amazed, and sent her in for another round of tests. The cancer was not growing, but the tumors were still there. They had no idea what prognosis to offer, but Mom knew exactly what to do. She decided her next needlework project should be larger and longer, so she chose an embroidered quilt. At first, it was to be a lap blanket. As the weeks turned to months, it became a quilt for a twin bed. After another year of good medical results and many completed squares, she decided to make it a queen-size quilt.

By the next year, the medical results were not so good. She started chemotherapy again, carrying a square from the quilt everywhere she went. Mom had never become great at needlework. Her sewing bag always spilled over with material and thread. Her clothes were covered in lint from the frayed edges of the squares. I am sure she spent a small fortune on needles, for she could never keep track of the one she was using.

Unfortunately, this time there was no medical miracle, and Mom quickly slipped away. In the ensuing chaos of her death and funeral, I stuck her sewing bag somewhere out of my way, forgotten.

A year later, I found the squares in a wadded up mess in a dark corner at the back of my closet. I took them out, running my fingers over the threads. I was touching the same fabric my mother's hands had so lovingly worked with. I found a quilter willing to assemble the squares and finish the quilt. Now, when I miss my mother, I wrap myself in her quilt, imagining the warmth of her arms wrapped around me in a comforting hug.

"For you, O Lord, will bless the righteous; with favor you will surround him as with a shield." Psalm 5:12

In Pieces

by Pam Whitley

It would be my first Christmas without my beloved husband. Thirty-two years with Mike; now I was alone. I found myself in a store buying flowers for his new tombstone as I watched others buying decorations for their Christmas trees. And I was sorting through the remnants of his life as others prepared for family get-togethers. I had to find something constructive to do in the midst of all the pain.

Walking into our closet, memories flooded my soul as I saw five of Mike's favorite shirts. When our son, Ben, was in college in the early '90s, the big flannel shirt became the fashion craze. I'd purchased two or three of those heavy 'big shirts,' for Ben for Christmas and every time he came home for the weekend, Mike would raid his closet and come out wearing one of those shirts. It became a joke. For the next few years after that, I bought Ben and Mike identical flannel shirts for Christmas. Ten years later, those shirts had continued to be Mike's favorites. In fact, as he started chemo and felt chilled much of the time, he lived in those shirts.

Taking the shirts off their hangers, I laid them in a corner of my sewing room. I knew I wanted to do something special with them but it took a few days to get the courage to cut into the shirts. Perhaps dismantling them bore too much of a parallel to what had happened to our lives.

When I finally did though, I found I could get several 8" wide strips from the front and the backs of the shirts as well as from the sleeves. Then I cut those strips into as many squares as I could, and soon I was sewing the squares back together and a quilt began to emerge.

As friends looked at my work in progress, they commented on what great choices I had made for my color combinations. Actually, I hadn't chosen anything. They were just all of his shirts, and now sewn together, they formed a beautiful color palette.

It seemed impossible to finish my project by Christmas, but

I was determined. For such a sad first Christmas without his father, there just had to be something special to give Ben, and I knew this was it. I asked God to give me the strength to complete my project, and day by day the quilt grew larger.

I sewed the labels of the shirts in some of the squares and deliberately cut strips with pockets so that it would always be evident that the quilt was made from shirts. To finish off the project, I bordered the quilt in navy and then I machine quilted the whole thing in a free hand motion style. At times I was able to turn my free hand motion movement into words. Within the quilt I wrote Whitley, 2003, Mike, Pam, Ben, Steph, Jack, and Will. I wanted this quilt to be a treasure for the generations to come. I envisioned that one day our grandsons would be searching the borders for the names woven into the design and Ben would share fondly the memories of his dad and the shirts.

On Christmas, as our son opened his gift, tears welled in his eyes and the look on his face and the hug I received was salve to my hurting heart. I knew God was at work using the shattered pieces of our lives to bring forth treasure in the darkness.

"Weeping may endure for a night, but joy comes in the morning." Psalm 30:5b

A "Good" Quilt Saved His Life

by Mary Brelsford

He wasn't sure what he saw, so quickly he ducked down under the quilt. Curiosity, and some fear, made him peek out again, screaming, "Mama, the geese are coming to get me!"

His mother quickly abandoned hanging more white sheets on the clothesline, realizing the wind-flapping sheets scared her sick child. She gathered him up from the porch shelter, wrapped in his quilt, and hurried into the house. Seated in a rocking chair, she held him close until his tears ceased and sleep came. She then laid him in bed, covered with his quilt.

After a short nap he awoke, patted the quilt, and murmured, "You saved my life! 'Good' quilt." His mother smiled.

This little boy became my dad. He was born in the mountains of Tennessee, where life was hard-scrabble, luxuries were few, but warm quilts covered the beds. When he told me this story, he still remembered the patches — Nine Patch — and truly believed quilts give special protection and comfort.

Needless to say, my mother, a Kentucky native, provided quilts for our beds, with the help of her mother and grandmother. Both were avid quiltmakers. Some of these quilts still give comfort to their progeny. This I know personally: quilts provide cherished memories, especially when I snuggle under a quilt and think of my dad. I also remember my grandmother pulling scraps from her basket, one by one, until a magical quilt appeared. My mother would say, "Now Mama, that's a 'good quilt'", and my grandmother would smile.

"I will both lie down in peace, and sleep; for You alone, O LORD, make me dwell in safety. Psalm 4:8

It All Started With a Pig

by Delores Ann Patton Rieck

Asthma restricted my physical activities when I was a young girl. At family gatherings I couldn't play outside with my siblings and cousins because I had trouble breathing. My great aunt Fannie taught me how to quilt as I sat in the bay window of her home, watching all the fun the other kids were having outside. The fabric and stitching were fascinating, but I yearned to join my friends in hide-and-seek, tether ball and red-rover games.

Grandmother Harriet entertained me by taking me material shopping every time she went. She patiently and lovingly instructed me as she transferred her love of textiles to me. She even gave me her old Singer treadle sewing machine.

Twenty years later I married Gary, who farmed and raised pigs while I continued teaching school in Burlingame, Kansas. One beautiful Sunday afternoon in April of 1965, we journeyed to Lawrence, Kansas to purchase a boar pig. Gary parked the car beneath a shade tree and said, "I'll be back in 30 minutes." The 30 minutes came and went and grew into 2 hours. Many thoughts raced through my mind as I sat and waited... and waited. With nothing to do, I had lots of time to make a plan. That day I made the commitment to start quilting in earnest, which was something I'd always wanted to pursue.

The Lord blessed me with asthma so I could enjoy a lifetime of quilting. Over the past 40 years, I have produced over 600 quilts of all sizes from miniature to king size. I created a quilt for every new baby in the family, graduate, wedding, anniversary or birthday gift. Each quilt is lovingly made and given with the knowledge that my quilting is a gift from the Lord.

Throughout my teaching career, I taught many children and adults how to quilt. For several years I have taught quilt classes in the local community school and through two quilt shops. Quilt guilds, church groups, senior citizens, and elementary schools often request my program, "Quilts that Tell a Story." My introduction always includes how the Lord blessed me with asthma, but how it really all started with a pig.

Ken's Comfort
by Carol Cutler

My husband, Ken, enjoyed dressing up to go to church. Most of the time, he chose slacks and a sport coat with an oxford shirt and complimentary tie. In the summer of 1997, Ken suffered a heart attack and passed away.

My dear friend, Sandi Patty, sang at his funeral and afterwards suggested that I save Ken's shirts and make a quilt of them. I put the thought in the back of my mind.

Several weeks later my daughters and I went through Ken's clothing to give to his brothers. I laid aside all of his oxford shirts... yellow, blue, burgundy stripe, blue stripe and yellow stripe, along with many white ones. I put them into a big black bag and stored them in the garage until I could decide what to do with them.

One of my friends at church was a quilter and agreed to make the quilt.

She chose a 12 inch Nine Patch pattern. Each of the nine small squares were cut from different colored shirts. Then she cut 12 inch white blocks to piece in between the colored Nine Patch squares. With the remaining white shirts, she pieced a border. She made one adorable pillow from four of the shirt pockets, and two other pillows trimmed with his buttons.

When I saw the finished product, I immediately called it "My Quilt that Comforts!" I feel a part of Ken is nearby... comforting me.

> *"Blessed be the... God of all comfort, who comforts us in all our tribulation, that we may be able to comfort those who are in any trouble, with the comfort with which we ourselves are comforted by God."* 2 Corinthians 1:4

Legacy Quilts Give Courage and Hope
by Carole Peery

As Margaret Garton tucked her six-year-old daughter Carole into bed, Carole begged, "Mommy, why did your Mommy and Daddy put you in an orphanage? Are you going to put me there if I'm bad?"

No, of course not honey," Margaret assured Carole. " We love you more than words can say. We would never think about giving you away. Is that why you've been so sad lately?"

"But why did you have to live in that old orphanage? Didn't your parents love you?"

"When I was two, my Daddy left us to find a job in another town and never came back," Margaret explained to her daughter. "My mama tried to support us, but couldn't earn enough to feed and clothe us. I remember how hard I cried when she said good-bye. The women in the Blinn House in Oklahoma City were very kind to me, but I missed my family so much."

"Life must have been very lonely and horrid without a Mommy and Daddy to love you. Did you ever take vacations?"

"Why yes. I cherished the summers and holidays I spent with my Grandma and Grandpa Gardner on their farm in Mustang, Oklahoma. Grandpa taught me how to fish, swim, garden and milk the cows. He even let me ride his big tractor. I'll never forget the smell of pumpkin and apple pies baking and the turkey roasting when Grandma let me help her fix Thanksgiving dinner. She tied her ruffled feed sack apron over the new dress she made me, but I still smeared butter and flour everywhere. In fact I still have Grandmas's recipe book that I'll give you when you get married. I always felt so special and loved in that safe, peaceful haven away from the orphanage."

"Tell me again how you met Daddy, and about your wedding."

So Margaret started in, "I graduated from Northeast High School in May of 1959 and was praying desperately for God to provide a Christian husband so I could live in a home of my own. I was singing in the choir at University Heights Baptist Church when I saw a handsome stranger walk through the door.

"He had piercing blue eyes and dark wavy hair, and my heart started thumping wildly. After the service I pushed my way through the crowds and introduced myself. He shook my hand and electricity tingled through every nerve of my body. We dated for two weeks and were married June lst. Grandpa walked me down the aisle to the rhythm of the Wedding March."

Margaret went on to add, "Grandmother Gardner presented me with an exquisitely handmade Double Wedding Ring quilt. It was my most prized possession because it brought back all the fond memories of the love and good times we shared on their Mustang farm. Then when you were born, she made a crib quilt for you."

"Can I see my quilt, Mamma? Where is it?"

"Unfortunately, growing up in an orphanage without individual mothering presented some real challenges for me as a newly-wed — like doing the laundry. I'll never forget cleaning Daddy's wool suit in the washer and dryer and the legs and sleeves shrinking six inches."

"I'll bet he was mad at you. Did he threaten to leave you too."

"Oh no, precious. He was a little disgruntled at first, but later chuckled about it."

"But where is the quilt your Grandma made you and where's my baby quilt?" Carole still wanted to know.

" I was getting to that. I washed both quilts one day and let them soak overnight in bleach to get them clean. The next morning after I turned the old Maytag washer dial to finish the agitating, rinsing and spinning cycle, I pulled the quilts out and they tore in shreds. The bleach had disintegrated the fabric. I was devastated! I cried so hard even your Daddy couldn't console me. That was the year after Grandma died so I knew I'd never get another one of her quilts to replace them. The quilts were all I had left to connect me with Grandma's love"

"How could you Mamma? And now I'll never have a quilt either," sobbed Carole.

Thirty years later Carole and her mother were given another chance. Aunt Helen surprised Carole with five quilts made by Margaret's Grandmother Gardner. Carole was elated, especially when she discovered that one was a Double Wedding Ring quilt. She immediately gave it to her overjoyed mother to replace the one the washer shredded. Tragically, this quilt was later stolen during Margaret's move to New Orleans. Carole gave her sister two quilts and kept a Dresden Plate and a navy and white overshot coverlet that her great, great grandmother wove of homespun wool and flax.

A few years later Carole called her Aunt Helen to thank her again for the quilts. "You'll have to come over to see," Carole told her aunt. "I've hung the Dresden Plate quilt on my living room wall and it adds such a warm and cozy feel. I like to envision the family members who wore the dresses and bonnets that were cut up for the quilt. The colors cheer me in my darkest moments and remind me of the red birds and flowers I see while reading my Bible out on the porch."

"How's your daughter Catherine doing?" Aunt Helen asked, taking Carole from her happy thoughts to a current heartache. "How long has she battled that brain cancer anyway?" Helen wanted to know.

"They diagnosed it ten years ago," Carole reminded her aunt, thinking how fast all the years had gone. "We were devastated and still struggle with her paralysis and blindness in one eye. The Doctor says she needs another surgery soon. But she's a straight A student in her Junior year of high school. I'm encouraging both daughters to sew and embroidery. Maybe someday we'll all learn to quilt together to create our own heirloom quilts to pass along to succeeding generations."

"Your family has certainly endured more that its share of tragedies," Helen commented, then asked, "Didn't your brother die when you were a baby?"

"Yes," Carole admitted he had. She thought about how her extended family has triumphantly overcome many, many heartaches. " I know now that family is the most important thing, apart from our relationship with God," she told Aunt Helen. "My legacy quilts give me comfort and confidence that I too can endure victoriously, just as they did. My past trials strengthen my faith in a loving, sovereign God, and give me courage to face each day with steadfastness and hope."

As her fingers caressed the beautiful reds, blues and yellows in the Dresden Plate she continued, "The quilts lift my spirits above unpleasant circumstances to focus on beauty instead of my misery on those difficult days. While contemplating decisions, I often concentrate on my great grandmother's quilt to get a broader eternal perspective. That's why I called you to thank you again for giving me her quilts. I am committed to preserving them for future generations as a noble heritage and badge of courage."

"Happy are those who are strong in the Lord, who want above all else to follow your steps. When they walk through the Valley of Weeping, it will become a place of springs where pools of blessings and refreshment collect after rains! They will grow constantly in strength..."
Psalm 84:5-7

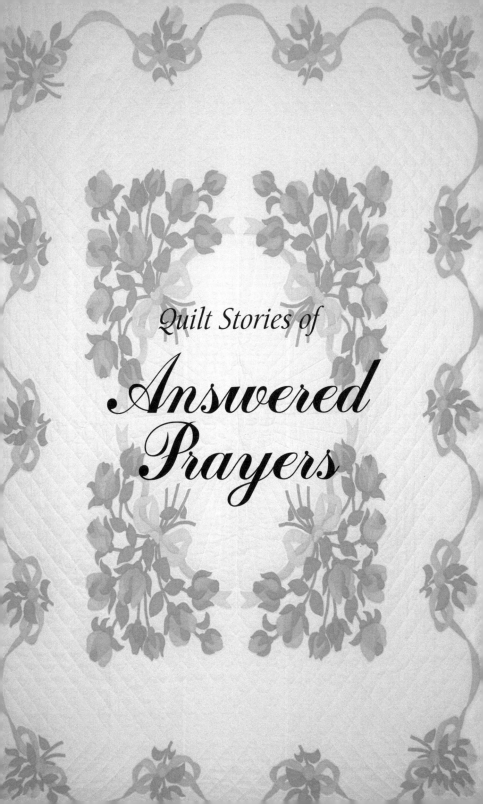

Quilt Stories of

Answered
Prayers

Remember

by Elaine Britt

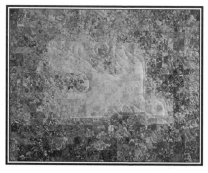

One hundred years — what a milestone! Still going strong, the church was looking forward to the upcoming celebration. Plans progressed as each area of ministry discussed how to contribute to the festivities. Not to be left out, my Prayer Ministry group initiated plans. While visiting many churches' prayer rooms to get ideas to furnish our own, I took a picture of a framed watercolor quilt with members' prayers.

At the next meeting, we were all drawn to the picture of the quilt and asked God if He wanted us to construct a smaller version for our prayer room? As months passed and we prayed, God directed us to develop a similar quilt, allowing church members to write prayers of thanksgiving and supplication concerning the church — past, present, and future — to be sewn inside.

At each meeting, we were "given" various scriptures pointing to the word "Remember" for the name of the quilt. I called Sharon, the textile artist who had made the watercolor quilt to obtain a price quote to undertake the task. Sharon offered gentle yet firm admonitions, "Your vision for this quilt is much smaller than God's. He wants to do great things during this 100-year milestone." Then she added, "I cannot possibly make this quilt top. Your church needs to own this project completely."

"But I know nothing about sewing, art or quilting, and don't know anyone who does," I replied.

"God has gifted the church with those who DO know how, and your mission is to find them," Sharon replied. "I will meet with you when you have 15-25 people and give you instructions. Pray continually through this and God will do the rest."

Within a week 25 people joined the effort. Sharon met with us and explained the design process. We decided on an Impressionistic theme using 2 inch x 2 inch squares, vibrant colors, and elements of nature. "Try to splash and swirl the squares," Sharon suggested. We had no idea what she meant until we started dealing with hundreds of squares that had a light and a dark side. As we moved the pieces here and there, the "splash and swirl" element assumed a life of its own.

Each gathering began with prayer, then friendly chatter commenced around the table: "Who wants to splash today?... Who feels called to swirl?... I'm seeing double... will someone switch swatches with me?... Whose turn is it to sew, and who wants the joy of ripping out our mistakes?" It was quickly obvious that each individual brought unique gifts to the group and only by working together as Christ's body — the church, would the project prosper.

Someone in the group shared a passage from Exodus 31:1-5, "See, I have chosen Bezalel... and I have filled him with the Spirit of God, with skill, ability and knowledge in all kinds of crafts to make artistic designs..." We all agreed that God was doing for us what he did for Bezalel, for we were splashing and swirling up a beautiful quilt top!

During the weeks of placing and piecing, prayers of members were collected, each written on pieces of cloth, to be sewn into the quilt. Over 200 were collected which was an inspiration and thrill to everyone.

Work completed, I delivered the quilt top to Sharon to be bordered and finished. She decided on blue as an appropriate border color referring to John 7:38, "He who believes in Me,... out of his heart will flow rivers of living water." I was marveling at how over 35 people had helped with praying, planning, designing, sorting, ironing, sewing, doing carpentry for framing, babysitting — over 600 hours altogether. After picking up the finished quilt several months later, I drove away jubilantly, praising God for making it all work.

Our church's Centennial Celebration was a huge success. We shared many fond memories and expressed optimism about the future. The Pastor presented our beautiful quilt in the morning worship service. Gasps of awe and surprise rippled throughout the sanctuary, bringing smiles to the faces of all who helped. It remains on display in the church hallway as a constant reminder to all of the blessed time spent in fellowship, and of God's faithfulness — regardless of our many swirls and splashes!

"Having then gifts differing according to the grace that is given to us, let us use them:" Romans 12:6a

The Oklahoma Twister Quilt

as told by Frances Thompson

Mike and Shirley Thompson were just sitting down to dinner that fateful Monday, May 3rd, 1999, when storm sirens started blaring. They flipped on T.V. to hear Gary England's weather warning; "This is an F5 tornado with wind speeds clocked at a record 318 miles/hour. All those in the Bridgecreek, Moore, south Oklahoma City and Del City areas should take shelter immediately. Multi-cell tornadoes have touched ground."

The Thompsons quickly grabbed pillows and blankets and jumped into their bathtub, and pulled a foam mattress over their heads. They waited and prayed as they held each other. They listened and guessed at what was flying past as torrential rains and howling winds ripped houses in their neighborhood apart, tossing them like matchsticks. Their own house started to creak and groan and then exploded. The next thing they saw was the ominous dark sky as they peeked from beneath their mattress. Occasional flashes of lightning illuminated debris flying by — a window fan, a porch swing, a chimney — just over their no longer roofed lodging.

After the eye of the storm passed over, Mike and Shirley climbed out of their bathtub to survey the damage. With the roof gone, everything was sopping wet. Every window had exploded. Broken glass and insulation were embedded in any remaining furniture. The garage was nowhere to be seen and their car was gone. The wind had even ripped up the driveway pavement. Pieces of their neighbor's two-by-fours and sheet metal now lay in what used to be Mike and Shirley's living room.

It was a miracle that they and the neighbors were even alive! They praised God, taking comfort that they still had each other. That was all that really mattered, they told themselves as they stepped over soggy photo albums and broken china. They were safe even though their house was beyond repair. "We can buy a new house," Mike kept telling Shirley. "It will be our new beginning together."

They remembered what Mike's Dad always said, "We are super-overcomer conquerors in all things in Christ Jesus." A preacher's kid, Mike had always been taught to count his blessings and trust God to provide for all his needs. This twister would reveal how much his dad had taught him.

As the next hours unfolded and Mike and Shirley further explored their chaos, they lamented the loss of irreplaceable family albums, school mementos and wedding pictures. Then they discovered the one treasure they valued above all others. "Mike," Shirley shouted, "here's the Wedding Sampler quilt your Mom made for us!" Mike's mom had made it by hand and given it to the couple for a wedding present. It had been on their bed since they were married. Only now it was filthy, embedded with asbestos and wrapped around the washer. And it was shredded in several places. "Maybe your Mom can mend it," Shirley said with hope and desperation. They wrapped the precious quilt and took it, along with a few necessities, to spend the night with Mike's parents.

"I can't promise anything," Frances Thompson said as she dubiously examined the damaged quilt, "but I'll give it my best shot! After all, it's a blue ribbon winner and survivor just like the two of you and certainly deserves my utmost attention and loving care. How ironic!" she said. "God must have a real sense of humor for the Oklahoma Twister block in the center of the quilt to be the only block that needs no mending."

Frances worked on the Twister quilt all summer long. She gingerly washed and rewashed the quilt to get the asbestos out. Then, tediously, she appliquéd 39 hearts to cover the tears. Fortunately she had squirreled away enough of the original fabric scraps to make the restorations unnoticeable.

In the meantime, Mike and Shirley bought a home in Norman and began settling in. Frances made duplicates of as many of the missing family pictures as she had and presented them, along with the restored quilt, as a housewarming gift.

"Wow!" Shirley exclaimed. "It looks better than new! Thank you so much for your gift of love and labor. You can't imagine how much we've missed our wedding quilt and how much it means to us that you cared enough to spend the long hours to recreate it." She gave her mother-in-law a happy hug and then said, "I'm twice blessed and will cherish it forever. It's going back on our bed to christen our new house and celebrate our new beginning. It will be our lasting remembrance of your love, God's protection, and the tornado that made us all realize how important family is."

> *"I will say of the LORD, 'He is my refuge and my fortress; my God, in Him I will trust.'.... He shall cover you with His feathers, and under His wings you shall take refuge;" Psalms 91:2,4 NKJ*

Friendship Quilt Connects Past with Present

as told by Mary Beth Walker

My aunt Sally from Atlanta and I were enjoying an afternoon of antiquing along the "May Avenue of Antiques" in Oklahoma City, when we entered a most unusual shop full of quilts. "What a bonanza!" exclaimed Sally, a quilter herself. "I feel like I've died and gone to Quilt Heaven!"

Sally and I were fondling all the quilts and reading the history of each, when our eyes met in shock. "This yellow and lavender calico quilt is from our hometown of Wynnewood," I exclaimed. "It was made and signed by the Ladies of the First United Methodist Church for their retiring preacher. It's dated 1939."

We checked for familiar names since we had both belonged to that church. "Wow," I said, pointing. "There's my Sunday school teacher's name. And here's our church organist."

"Look at this," Sally whispered, almost breathless. "It's your mom's name in the bottom corner."

"I've got to buy this quilt, no matter what the cost. My husband will kill me, but it's the only link we might have to connect with Mom now that Alzheimer's is stealing her mind. Maybe I can put it in layaway and get it out in time for her birthday," I said.

"That's a great idea!" Sally agreed. "I've read that often a familiar object from the past will trigger memories."

So, I put what cash I could down on the quilt and prayed for God to provide the rest so my husband wouldn't even have to find out. God was faithful with an unexpected windfall from Christmas gifts — just enough to pay off the balance a week before Mom's birthday. I rushed down to collect the quilt, wrapped it in a pretty box with a huge red bow and delivered it and a cake the next day to celebrate Mom's 85th birthday.

I quizzed Mom after she ripped open the box, "Does this look familiar?"

There was an awkward silence as tears rolled down her

stunned face. Finally she gained her composure and spoke clearly for the first time in nine months. Pointing to the calicos she beamed while she explained, "That's my work dress I made from feed sacks. And this is from Dad's dress shirt. The pink gingham was the dress I stitched for you when you were in the first grade. Then Mom searched the bottom corner and she asked somewhat puzzled, "What's my name doing down here?"

"Do you recognize any of the other names, Mom?" I asked. For the next two days, we reminisced about all the wonderful times we had shared as a family in Wynnewood. We were overflowing with thanksgiving to God for giving us this special quilt that triggered all those happy memories that bonded us together once again in love. God in His mercy had provided the means through Mama's quilt for me to connect with her one last time before He took her home.

"I remember the days of old; I meditate on all Your works;" Psalm 143:5

The Brag Book
by Helen Upton Earhart

"Before we stopped in Safad, Israel, I noticed that you were showing ladies on the bus pictures of the quilts you've made. Could I look at your photo album?" the woman seated next to me asked. " I'm a quilter too."

"I'd love to share the pictures and stories, especially with a fellow quilter," Helen said as she dug into the depths of her enormous black bag. After emptying the entire contents onto her lap, she threw up her hands in alarm. "Oh no! It can't be! At the last souvenir shop I took out my Brag Book to get my billfold to pay for one little thimble. I must have left it on the counter.

"Tiki, can you please turn this bus around?" Helen pleaded between sobs. "I've lost my Brag Book and it contains my life's history of quilting. We can't possibly go on without it."

"Sorry lady. I wish I could help you but we've got a schedule to keep and we're already late. I'm sure the shop owner will mail your book to you," Tiki said, not even looking at Helen in his rearview mirror and not slowing down one whit.

"But I transferred all the photos into a new album to bring on this trip and I forgot to put my name in it. I'll never see it again if you don't go back right now."

I was sick! Most of the quilts had been given away as gifts. There was no way I could get pictures of all 83 quilts again. I prayed desperately that somehow God would perform a miracle and make the album mysteriously appear.

Almost a year later, the phone rang. It was someone from *Quilter's Newsletter Magazine* asking if I had lost a photo album in Israel. Joan Koslan-Schwartz, owner of Needle's Point Studio in Vienna, Virginia had been to the same shop I had in Safad. The proprietor asked if she would take the album back to the United States to see if she could locate the owner. Joan called *Quilter's Newsletter Magazine* and told the editor, Bonnie Leman, that the only real identification in this Brag

Book was a photo of the label on the back of a Sunbonnet Sue quilt. The woman at *Quilter's Newsletter Magazine* told Joan that they would try, but sounded doubtful. All their subscribers are listed by zip code. Then Bonnie Leman's industrious niece went to her computer and found a subscriber named Helen Earhart. The subscription editor from the magazine called Joan and then me, and I received the book within a week. I was elated!

One month later I opened my *Quilter's Newsletter Magazine* and found that Bonnie Leman had written an article in her "The Needle's Eye" telling the story about my Brag Book.

Each time I get out my album, I praise God for answering my prayers. I tell the story when I teach and speak at quilt guilds, and jokingly say that it was a painful way to get my name in *Quilter's Newsletter Magazine*.

> *"Continue earnestly in prayer, being vigilant in it with thanksgiving;" Colossians 4:2a*

Pieces of Love

by Lynda Stephenson

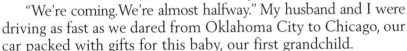

"They're taking her into surgery," my son-in-law, Neil, told me over my cell phone. "She's in extreme danger."

"What do the doctors think?" I asked.

"They don't know. But she's too weak, too tired to push any longer. She's been in hard labor for 18 hours." His voice broke. "A caesarean is all they can do now."

"We're coming. We're almost halfway." My husband and I were driving as fast as we dared from Oklahoma City to Chicago, our car packed with gifts for this baby, our first grandchild.

Months earlier, when our daughter Amy announced her pregnancy, we were ecstatic. But we were also frightened, because Amy suffers from a blood disorder, a low platelet count. I worried constantly.

Although I rarely sew, with a neighbor's help I started a quilt for this special grandbaby. My friend and I selected a child's crazy quilt pattern and bought colorful fabrics with tiny patterned figures. We used mostly yellows and greens, which would work well for either a boy or a girl, since Amy and Neil wanted the sex of their child to remain a surprise. In my fear for our daughter, I wasn't the least bit concerned about the child's gender. I only hoped and prayed that the baby would be healthy and our daughter would survive childbirth.

Working on that quilt, I learned a valuable lesson. Women through the centuries have made quilts not only to keep their families warm, and to create lovely works of art; they've also quilted to calm themselves from worry and fear. I finished the quilt before the baby was due, and then... we waited.

Finally, Neil called and asked us to come. "Dear God," my husband said, after I hung up. We quickly loaded the car, including the child's quilt and the many gifts we couldn't stop from buying, and headed north. We drove in silence, both unable to speak without breaking down, both trying to be brave for each other. Not knowing what we might have to face, we were filled with dread as we walked into the Chicago hospital.

But in the maternity ward we found a wonderful surprise — a weepy father, a healthy, exhausted mother, and a tiny, red-faced granddaughter.

From her crib, she looked up at us sharply, as if to say, "What took you so long?"

"This is the cutest little kid I ever saw," my husband cried.

"Her name is Sophia," my daughter said. "She's perfect. Our little miracle."

Sophia doesn't use the quilt I made. Since her mother thinks it's a work of art, she hung it on a wall in the nursery. This past summer, we redecorated the room, painted the walls and bought three-year-old Sophia a set of "big girl" furniture. When we re-hung the quilt, she said to me, "Oh, Muffy! Isn't my room beautiful?"

Next summer Sophia will have a baby sister. She's coming from a Chinese orphanage. Like so many others, this child was probably placed in a box and left in a train station or perhaps in a park by a mother who couldn't keep her. No doubt the mother hid and watched as the baby was discovered and taken away to a safe place. Amy and Neil have completed the paperwork necessary to adopt this child, and again we have all begun the long process of waiting.

It's time for me to make another quilt. My neighbor has promised to help me make something symbolic and meaningful for this second grandchild. We plan to piece a traditional Log Cabin, made from fabrics with tiny oriental symbols and figures combining a historical American design and a Chinese motif, a spectacular quilt for a spectacular little girl.

As I piece the quilt this winter, I'll think of my granddaughters: the miracle baby who was wanted so badly her mother was willing to die to give her life, and the Chinese child, crowded in a crib with others, whose poor mother wanted her to have a life so badly she gave her away. I imagine that someday my grandchildren will discuss these quilts and what they stand for for both of them — the fierceness of a mother's love.

> *"For God so loved the world that He gave His only begotten Son, that whoever believes in Him should not perish but have everlasting life." John 3:16*

El Roi... The God Who Sees

by Kelly Weir

I had committed to a day of prayer and fasting. During that day I prayed, Lord, please show yourself to me in a new way. God didn't wait long to answer my prayer! The very next morning, He began to reveal Himself to me in a way I never would have imagined.

I planned to take my daughter Lindsay's handmade quilt to the dry cleaners and so set it out by the front door. When I returned home from taking my two daughters to school, I realized that I had forgotten the quilt. It was not, however, where I had put it. I called my husband Russ at work and asked, "Honey, did you put the trash out this morning?"

Pleased with himself, because he does not often remember our trash day, he replied "Yes, I sure did."

My heart stopped. I had placed Lindsay's quilt in a white kitchen trash sack. It wasn't in the trash can, but Russ had assumed it was trash. I was sick! Russ' mother had made this beautiful quilt for Lindsay, my 13-year-old daughter, and it was on its way to the trash dump.

I quickly called my neighbor Susan. Her husband worked in the executive offices of Waste Management. Jim knew exactly who to call at the company that serviced our area. In fact, he called their offices and explained the mishap.

My friend Tammy came by my house, so I jumped in her car, and we set out to look for the neighborhood trash truck. We found a truck at the end of the street, but it wasn't the right one. That driver radioed to the correct truck, and directed us to it in a nearby neighborhood. The driver of our truck callously told us he was "so sorry, but this wasn't the first time someone had thrown away something accidentally."

I was tearful. I couldn't imagine having to tell my mother-in-law that her son had thrown away the quilt she had so lovingly made.

About that time, Susan called on the car phone. "Get the

truck number," she said.

Tammy and I went back to the truck. God had softened the man's heart and he now listened more empathetically to my pleas and told us where the dump was. It was impossible to pull anything out of the truck's trash compactor. We'd have to come to the dump. So I called the company, got estimated arrival times and directions, and called Russ. He agreed to clear his schedule for the day and meet me at the dump.

I began calling my prayer warriors. Pam was wonderful and told me "Kelly, El Roi, the God who sees, knows exactly where Lindsay's quilt is and we will pray you find it."

About that time, Kristin, Lindsay's twin sister, called from school. This was unusual, but very much God's timing. Kristin is one of my mightiest prayer warriors. Without giving details, I asked her to pray. She assured me she would.

Russ and I met at the dump, clear on the other side of town before 11:30 a.m. when the truck was to arrive. It was an unusually warm day and didn't smell too wonderful. We waited and waited and waited. The truck never came.

Shortly after 3 p.m. I had to leave for a prior commitment. I knew the chances of finding Lindsay's quilt undamaged were very slim. I felt even less confident that it would be found if I left. I was concerned that the truck driver would not be as persistent if I was not there. However I continued to pray and to petition El Roi, the God who sees, and drove home to Edmond.

On my way home I called a friend. I told her about my day. She said "Kelly, you have no idea how many times I've prayed to El Roi, the God who sees, to help me find things I've misplaced!" I couldn't believe it. Two people had used this name for God to me in the same day. It was a name I had not known before.

Meanwhile, Russ maintained his post at the dump. When our trash truck arrived, it dumped more than ten tons of trash, creating a rank pile of garbage approximately six feet high and 20 feet wide. "Ok," said our driver, "let's see. Your addition is Danforth Farms; that should be right about here." He indicated an area about two-thirds of the way down the long pile. "What kind of trash bag was it in? White, with a red tie? OK."

Moving closer, he pulled out a black bag and repeated, "Yep, just about here."

Russ pointed to a nearby white patch of plastic. "It was a bag like that one."

With his gloved hand, our driver reached into the jumbled pile and pulled out our quilt. Both men were stunned. They were each sure we'd never retrieve it.

Minutes later, Russ called to tell me the good news. I was overjoyed. Amazingly, there was only one tiny tear on the back side of the beautiful off-white quilt. My friend Pam McKenzie patched it with an embroidered piece of fabric that commemorated our experience with these words, "January 30, 1998, El Roi, The God Who Sees."

That day I learned to never, ever put anything that I don't want thrown away in a trash bag. More importantly, God revealed Himself to me in a new way. I learned that He is El Roi, the God who sees. Our omnipresent God is there and His eyes are not shut. He is not asleep, slumbering, or unaware of our circumstances. He sees!

"I will lift up my eyes to the hills--from whence comes my help? My help comes from the LORD,"
Psalms 121:1-2

Grapes of Wrath Yield Treasures

by Jean Dani

It was 105 degrees that summer day of 1935, when I saw a sight I'll never forget. I was six years old and fetching eggs when a flock of mismatched birds landed on the parched ground that had been our vegetable garden before heat seared and shriveled every last zucchini and tomato. These birds were agitated and clearly exhausted. I looked at the sky and screamed to Mama as I ran into our small frame farmhouse south of Cordell, Oklahoma, "Mama, Mama, a huge black cloud is coming again."

"Quick," she shouted at me, "ring the dinner gong to call the others in from the fields. Every minute counts." Already Mama was reaching for a quilt. "Then run right back in here and help me drape this table. We'll get under our tent to protect our lungs from flying dirt."

Within ten minutes the sky was completely black with howling winds and cutting sand and dust that could choke the life from any creature. Soon the whole family was huddled beneath the quilts and praying that God would spare the cows, pigs and chickens and what was left of the crop, one more time.

Such was life in the Dust Bowl Days of western Oklahoma, our tent days and nights repeated over and over. That natural hardship combined with the Great Depression, was made worse by the fact that my dad was ill and unable to work during most of my childhood. But Daddy could do one thing. I remember the beautiful String quilt he made by hand my first year of school. During Dad's convalescence, he gained a feeling of accomplishment by creating beauty from cast-off scraps of fabric. And the family gained needed warm bedding. Piecing and quilting also became Dad's therapy — a quiet time when he could pray and meditate on God's promises to provide. He dreamed of the time he and his family could join the thousands of other farmers in their flight for jobs and a better life in California.

Since Mother was forced to do most of the farm work, she didn't have much leisure time for needlework. But I remember the beautiful Friendship quilt she made with all the signed quilt blocks of church friends and family. All the neighbor ladies gathered at our house to complete her Friendship quilt. We prepared a feast to celebrate, cleared away the mess, then lowered the quilting frame from the ceiling. Needles flew amidst much gossip and laughter. By the end of the long day, the quilt was finished and I had learned to quilt just from watching. The ladies graciously allowed me to put in the last few stitches just to appease my incessant requests to help.

In those days of little money or means, entertainment revolved around school and church activities. Every summer a visiting minister came for an all-day revival under the brush arbor. We enjoyed singing and praising God for His faithfulness. Afterwards we shared a potluck feast and a watermelon feed that climaxed the unforgettable event.

In 1943 during World War II, Dad's dream for a better life in California became a reality. We moved to Sacramento. That's where I met my husband, Charles, who had just returned from the war. We married in 1947 and Charles' mom made us a beautiful wedding quilt, which I still treasure.

Within that barren landscape of the Great Depression and Oklahoma's Dust Bowl Days were other treasures which I hold dear. Ours was a story of courage, hope and love in the midst of poverty and struggles against drought and endless dust that was as much a part of life as sunshine and air. The hardships bound our family together in unity and dependence on God's daily provision, making us stronger in our faith, able to withstand any heartache.

> *"Through the LORD's mercies we are not consumed, because His compassions fail not. They are new every morning. Great is Your faithfulness. 'The LORD is my portion,' says my soul. "Therefore I hope in Him!" Lamentations 3:22-24*

A Blanket of Prayers

by Dorothy Palmer Young

When I learned that my son Daniel was to be deployed to Iraq, I immediately set up an e-mail prayer group. I invited my friends, and those I knew who were friends of Dan and his wife Lori to sign-up for e-mail prayer updates about his needs. The response was heartening. So many friends, and even strangers, offered to pray.

Working out at the YMCA one day, I encountered my friend Sandy. She quickly agreed to pray for Daniel. Then she volunteered, "In my church, Dorothy, when we are blanketing someone in prayer, we present them with an actual blanket we have made. It's a physical reminder of all the prayers going to God on their behalf."

I loved the idea. By the time I completed my workout, I had mentally completed a rough design of a prayer blanket for Dan and Lori. In Iraq, traveling light, Dan wouldn't have room to lug around an extra blanket with his gear, even a small one. Waiting in Germany, however, Lori would not only have room in their little house, but room in her empty arms as well. A warm, cuddly, comforting blanket would be perfect.

Soon I met with Lori's mom, Sheryl, to talk. "Let's make a prayer blanket together for Dan and Lori," I suggested. "Wouldn't it be great if the people praying for Dan's mission and safety could actually sign it?" She loved the idea, too.

That's when the blanket became a cream and gold colored nine-square quilt. By using squares, Sheryl and I could each take one or more of the 12-inch squares with us everywhere we went. Hooped and ready, each broadcloth square was soon filled with the autographs of "pray-ers." From across the country we received signatures by mail and e-mail. These too were traced onto squares.

Dan left Germany for Iraq in early February. For weeks I sent out prayer updates, and gathered names on the quilt pieces. When Dan first left home to join the army ten years earlier, my husband Bob had chosen a Bible verse for him. For all that time, Bob closed every correspondence to his son with his special scripture. I knew that verse must be the centerpiece of the prayer blanket; it had such deep meaning for us all. Psalm 20:7, "Some trust in chariots and some in horses, but we trust in the name of the Lord our God." Everyday we entrust ourselves and our son to God. That is at the center of our prayers, and would be embroidered at the center of the "blanket."

By mid-March, Sheryl and I had collected over 200 signatures. It was time to assemble the prayer blanket. I joined the squares, added the filler, backing, and border. With some simple hand tying, the blanket was complete. I snuggled up to its soft flannel backing and traced around the handwritten signatures with my finger. How good these friends were to pray for Dan and Lori. I tenderly folded and boxed the finished quilt-blanket for a special journey.

Lori's mom and dad traveled to Germany to visit Lori. They took that precious gift to deliver in person. At home in Oklahoma, I imagined Lori's reaction. I cried as I thought about the moment she would open the package.

I soon heard from Lori. "Thank you so much for the beautiful quilt," she wrote. "It means a lot to know we have so many praying for us... I e-mailed a picture of the quilt to Dan and told him about it. You guys are great. Sometimes I just sit in my chair with the blanket wrapped around me. I really do feel like Dan and I both are blanketed in prayer."

I'm glad I could be a part of creating something so meaningful to Lori and Dan, as he served his country in Iraq. It wasn't just a gift that friends and strangers had given to Lori and Dan. It was also a great blessing to me! With every voice of "Yes, please let me sign the quilt; I'm praying for them every day," I was encouraged.

Dan safely completed his tour in Iraq. He and Lori moved to Italy for another assignment. The prayer blanket hangs in a place of honor on a quilt rack in their new home. It will forever have a place of honor in my heart. Not only does it represent the many prayers for Dan and Lori, it represents the many friends who ministered to my heart as well.

" Some trust in cheriots and some in horses, but we trust in the name of the Lord our God" Psalm 20:7

God Loves Quilts Too

by Judy Howard

One rainy September night in 1992, my husband and I were jarred out of our dreams by the jangling of the bedside telephone. "Who'd be calling at this hour?" I grumbled. Then I heard the words we dreaded most from our security system provider, "You have an alarm going off at 1411 North May."

Hurriedly we threw on clothes and broke all speed limits driving to my Buckboard Antique Quilt Shop. All the way I reminded God, "Lord those are your quilts. If you want them stolen, it's all right by me. You're in total control. Although I don't understand what's going on, I'm trusting you and I refuse to let Satan terrorize me with fears and anxiety."

An unexpected calm surrounded me as I pulled up in front of the shop, despite the flashing red lights from three squad cars which greeted us as we scrambled out of our car. Tentatively, I turned the key in the lock and flipped on all the lights in my familiar little shop so that I could lead the entourage of policemen through each room. We all gasped when we reached the back room. Burglars had broken in through the back window, and shattered glass covered the floor and every nearby surface. They'd pushed over an 1800's pine cupboard in front of the window, spewing its contents everywhere. Every one of my prized red and white quilts that had adorned the walls in that room was gone.

As the police drove away, Bill and I began inventorying the missing quilts — my Amish Sunshine and Shadows, Civil War Log Cabin Barn Raising, 1800's Democrat Rose, Irish Chain, Wedding Ring, Bethlehem Star, etc. I kept repeating, "God, you are in control. This business is Yours along with all my belongings. I am just Your steward." I believed the words each time I said them. Then I'd discover something else that was broken or ruined; and I'd try to keep from bursting into tears of anger and self-pity, thinking of all the lost time, energy and resources that went in to amassing that collection of highly desirable quilts. After an hour of cleaning up the mess and securing the window, we were shocked when someone tapped on the front glass, scaring us half out of our wits. But then the kind policeman handed us three stacks of muddy red and white quilts, all present and accounted for. Nine blocks away, the officers had apprehended two men driving a white pickup with the truck bed overflowing with empty beer bottles... and God's quilts. You've never heard so much celebrating and praising the Lord. The officers even joined in with a few "hallelujahs". It was a real hootenanny!

"Doesn't that just make you love the Lord even more to see how good He is?" I asked the baby-faced officer, who looked too young to be up late chasing burglars. "God must have loved those quilts as much as I do." Then I went on to explain something I believe. "God was testing me to see if those quilts had become my idol and were more important to me than He was. He rewarded me for my obedience in seeking Him first and for yielding to Him my rights to those quilts."

As we turned out the lights and locked the door, knowing no thief could take what really mattered, I thanked the officer. And I told him, "Just as Romans 8:28 promised, God turned this bad thing to good to strengthen my faith and to teach me to trust Him more." And with that, Bill and I drove home, leaving the store in the dark, and in the capable hands of God, its true owner.

> "And we know that all things work together for good to those who love God, to those who are the called according to His purpose." Romans 8:28

A Tiny, Enormous Miracle

by Tricia Lehman

I walked into the living room the other night to unstrap my two-month old grandson from his infant seat, and he grinned at me. No one had warned me. I didn't know he had learned this incredible trick to steal his grandmother's heart. Of course, I reacted like any red-blooded grandma would — I squealed and I laughed and I cried. Seeing his beautiful smile reminded me so much of the baby's dad, my son Colin. He was born with the disposition of a sunbeam — happy, smiley, and full of laughter.

Even after my husband died tragically and I later remarried, Colin never caused any trouble. His ready smile made it easy for him to get along with almost everyone. Unfortunately that amazing smile got him into trouble at age 15 when he discovered it was an effective tool for attracting girls. A battle over his dating raged for a year until we decided he could date, but without our financial support except for clothing, room and board.

Colin agreed to those terms and worked hard over the next years to pay for his car, insurance and entertainment. He dated his way through his final years of high school with a new girl each year. We did our best to be polite and friendly while we desperately prayed. However, in his senior year he met Heather who was a year younger. During Colin's first semester of college, he and Heather told us she was pregnant. Disappointed, sad, and trying not to scream "We told you so," we gave counsel. We suggested adoption placement and marriage, and we offered our unconditional support.

When we discovered a short time later that Heather had scheduled an abortion, we were devastated. All our worries about lost scholarships and wasted youth faded into the background in this life and death situation. Our family stormed heaven with prayers. We had no legal rights or recourse. Only God could intervene.

Those weeks of waiting were agony. I spent the time doing

what any good quilter would do — I made a quilt for my unborn grandchild. For every stitch there was a tear. For every tear there was a matching prayer.

I sewed, not knowing if a baby would ever sleep tight under that blankie. It had to be made anyway. If nothing else, my quilt would serve as a lasting memorial of a life taken and a grandmother's broken-hearted love.

The quilt label read: "'1 love the Lord, for He heard my voice; He heard my cry for mercy. Psalm 116:1' For my precious unborn grandchild, With love, prayers and tears, Gran." I presented the quilt to Heather, and she patiently allowed me to read her all the Bible verses that mentioned unborn babies.

We waited and waited, until finally the news came. God answered our prayers. Our grandchild would live. Heather cancelled her appointment for an abortion.

The next months were not easy as we watched our son make some very immature decisions and almost break the heart of a strong, courageous young woman. With time and much counselling, Colin and Heather both realized that they yearned to be committed to each other and to the baby they had made. After a wedding and a high school graduation, Steven was born.

Now, the little guy was grinning at me from his infant seat. As I lifted the baby into my arms for a snuggle and kissed his precious, bald Charley-Brown-head, my heart swelled with gratitude and overwhelming love for this tiny, enormous miracle.

> "Can a woman forget her nursing child, and not have compassion on the son of her womb? Surely they may forget, yet I will not forget you. See, I have inscribed you on the palms of My hands;" Isaiah 49:15-16

N.Y.C. Reporter Incarcerated in Quilt Shop

On June 10th, 1995, I unlocked the door of my Buckboard Antique and Quilt Shop and waded in. The five inches of rain we'd received in eight hours had caused flash flooding and power outages, and when I hit the switch in the store, nothing. Fortunately, Kathy Herndon, my sweet 70-year-old Sunday school teacher, had been drilling into my thick skull the importance of thanking God for everything — from the nit-picking irritations to the full-blown crises of everyday life. It was a lesson I'd been trying hard to learn. It could have been worse, I reasoned as I rushed to Home Depot to buy the last wet and dry vacuum in town. "Thank you Father it wasn't a fire."

With temperatures in the 90's and no air conditioning, the aroma of storm sewer and wet antique wool rugs in my 80-year-old eternally musty shop was overpowering. After dragging outside a water-logged 9'x12' oriental carpet, a room-size hand hooked rug and countless other soggy smaller rugs, and sucking up the standing water with my new purchase, I was exhausted. Fumbling around in the dark for a couple of hours, I tried to salvage whatever I could that floated or squished beneath my feet. Finally I locked the shop and took a lunch break, vowing not to return until my electricity was restored.

When I returned to the shop an hour or so later, I was shocked to find two frantic, exquisitely dressed women pounding on the door to get out. "Are you alright?" I asked as I unlocked the door. "How in the world did you get in here?"

"I guess you didn't hear us while you were running the vacuum," replied one of the ladies as she wiped the sweat from her forehead with her silk animal-print scarf.

"I am so very sorry. You must have been miserable with this stifling heat and stench. Please accept my humblest apologies. I had no idea anyone was in here."

"Oh, no harm done," she said and went on to tell me that she was Laura Palmer and her friend's name was Beth Rowton. "We actually enjoyed prowling around. I even found a floral chenille bedspread I'd like to purchase." While she dug through her purse, she explained that she was in Oklahoma City from New York City to give a speech about her book, Shrapnel in the Heart about letters and poems left at the Vietnam Veterans Memorial.

Over the years, Laura has become a treasured customer and an avid quilt collector. She also played a vital role in interviewing and writing Nancy Levings' quilt story that aired on N.B.C. a year after Laura's time of "incarceration" in my shop.

I've since come to realize that God was working behind the scene in a rather unorthodox way through my disaster. About the same time, Nancy was praying for funds to educate her autistic son. God provided those funds through the help of Laura Palmer and many others. Had I not been rejoicing in God's sovereign love, learning to trust Him to turn this flood to good, I would have missed His sense of humor and His blessings of a great new customer and friend. We all had a good laugh about my locking the N.Y.C. Television Journalist in that day. You'll have to admit it makes a great story, especially for a professional writer.

> *"Rejoice always, pray without ceasing, in everything give thanks; for this is the will of God in Christ Jesus for you."*
> *1 Thessalonians 5:16-17*

The Wedding Quilt

by Nancy Levings

"There's just no way we can raise $6500 to send Matthew to that Son-Rise Institute back east," Larry Levings vehemently retorted. "Plus you'd have the expense of airplane tickets, motel and meals for two weeks. You know we have Katy's college tuition to pay, and my truck's broken down again. The answer is no — positively no!"

"But what will become of our 13-year-old son if we don't do something now," Nancy sobbed. "I can't handle him when he throws one of his tantrums. They say teenage years for autistic children can be a total nightmare for everyone concerned. I just know if we can get him into the right program, the genius inside him can be unleashed and he'll bloom like a beautiful rose. We've got to try!

"There's got to be a way to raise the money. The only things of value we have are nine nanny goats and lots of unpaid bills. Wait a minute... What about my great grandmother's Wedding quilt? It's just taking up space in the cedar chest. I've always loved it as my most priceless treasure. But I love Matthew even more and am determined to give him this chance to blossom to his full potential. What do you think honey?"

"But that legacy quilt has always meant so much to you," Larry said as he reached out to comfort her. "Are you sure you can sacrifice it? It would take a major miracle to raise all the money you're going to need."

"I could take it to Sarah Wilson and see if the United Methodist Church of Hooker, Oklahoma, could auction it off or something. Maybe we could at least raise enough for the $1500 down-payment to Son-Rise and pray that God provides the rest."

The next day Nancy showed Sarah her beautiful appliquéd quilt made in 1870. "Look," exclaimed Nancy as she opened the <u>Oklahoma Heritage Quilt book</u>. "Here's the picture of the quilt taken by the Heritage Quilt Group when they came out to document quilts in Guymon. It says, 'The family Bible records in German that this quilt was made near Cedar Creek,

Nebraska, as a wedding gift for the owner's paternal great-grandmother, Elizabeth Nolting Volk. The Star with Tulips was quilted at a quilting bee by friends and family. Elizabeth brought her wedding quilt to Oklahoma Territory in 1903 when her family moved to a farm near Renfrow.' We could even throw in the book. What do you think?" Nancy asked.

"I'm going to Oklahoma City next week. Why don't I take it along and at least get it appraised. I've got a Yellow Pages Directory right here. Let's see... Here's a Judy Howard at Buckboard Antiques and Quilts. I could take it to her and see what she says," suggested Sarah.

When Judy saw the beautiful quilt and heard the story, she was deeply moved and volunteered to try to sell it or use it as a fund-raiser if Nancy would agree to leave it. She gave freely of her services, advising the best strategies for promoting Matthew's story and used her contacts to spread the word.

On February 13, a British M.D. and quilt collector with a tender heart admired the beautiful quilt. After hearing the sad tale, she offered to buy the quilt and give it back to Nancy. The next day Judy showed the quilt to another customer who actually handed her a check for $500 to send to Nancy. Over the next two months, customers continued to show their generosity to help Matthew.

This project took on a life of its own. Nancy wasn't aware of just how much it was touching people until February 25, 1996, when she opened a letter from Judy containing checks totaling $1500. "Praise the Lord! How did she know this was all I needed to make the down payment to the Son-Rise Institute?" Nancy said as she excitedly shared the great news with Larry. "It's going to happen! Our little Matthew is going to get his chance to shine. God is somehow going to make it happen. I just know it."

Meanwhile, Judy called Laura Palmer, the New York City TV journalist who was incarcerated in her shop the summer before and explained Nancy's plight. Laura immediately arranged to come with a video crew to Buckboard and to Hooker to do interviews. On March 26, Laura and all the TV cameras, equipment, and lights arrived. Nancy's quilt story aired on the Television News Network in August of 1996 just when the Levings needed the encouragement the most. Larry had just lost his job and their home was in serious need of repairs following a damaging storm. God proved once again that He does answer our prayers exceedingly abundantly above anything we can dream or ask. He provided Matthew almost twice the amount of the original goal of $6500 for his on-going personalized education.

Nancy's quilt served a higher purpose than existing as a much cherished keepsake. It provided a higher legacy — the means for starting Matthew on the road to change. His progress includes learning social skills, developing speech, and being able to display the loving person inside, which is much more than they ever imagined possible. Nancy's purpose in writing this story is to express her appreciation and gratitude to all quilt lovers who are so compassionate and caring. "Thank you from the bottom of my heart!"

> *"Now to Him who is able to do exceedingly abundantly above all that we ask or think, according to the power that works in us, to Him be glory..." Ephesians 3:20-21a*

Believing God for a Winter's Harvest

by Judy Howard

Saturday morning I hit the pavement running, pursuing my dream of finding that illusive perfect quilt by "estate saleing". It takes perseverance to overcome the discouragement of many futile estate attempts. Occasionally God rewards me though with a jewel, and then it's my job to give it back to Him to multiply for His Kingdom, like the boy's fishes and loaves.

After signing in on the estate sale list and waiting semi-patiently for 30 minutes, the uniformed policeman finally announced my name. I entered the huge Quail Creek home, complete with indoor pool, and elbowed my way up the winding staircase to the bedroom. A real curiosity captivated me. A circular quilt attached to a hinged 42 inch round 5/8 inch thick piece of plywood hung on the wall. Some patient quilter had appliquéd clusters of soft faded lavender grapes and leaves on an embroidered vine with a center grape leaf wreath onto a gray background.

"What do you suppose this was used for?" I asked the equally puzzled helper as she wrote up my ticket. "I've never seen a round quilt before, have you?" She was as perplexed as I was as I excitedly lifted down the quilt. I hauled the awkward 15 pound prize all over the mansion, and gingerly navigated my way through the countless fragile breakables and hoards of people. I breathed a sigh of relief and massaged my aching muscles as I set down my treasure and waited in line to pay.

"Can you please tell me who made this quilt and what you know about it?" I asked the cashier, as I wrote my check.

"All I know is that the owner of this estate is Mr. Dry who founded Sheplar's Western Wear stores," the cashier told me.

"It's really quite beautiful and unusual, isn't it!" My sentiments exactly. I rushed home to more closely examine my find.

The half inch crosshatch quilting was museum quality at 12 stitches per inch with leaf patterns around the outer border. A tiny name and date were embroidered on the border. On the back penned on a muslin tag was "Francie Ginocchio, Stevens Point, Wisconsin. Title: Winter's Harvest."

"What an appropriate title for such bleak, dismal colors," I told my husband. "But nobody harvests grapes or anything else in the winter. Do they? What on earth does Winter's Harvest mean?"

"Everything is pretty dead in the winter," he replied. "Maybe you could research the artist on the internet."

I rushed to my computer and typed in Francie Ginocchio. I learned that she was a famous quilt artist, teacher and lecturer and decided to phone her.

When I reached Francie, I told her about buying her fabulous quilt and asked her the meaning of the title. "Oh, I just loved working with those soft faded lavenders and grays which reminded me of winter, so I called it Winter's Harvest. There was no significance deeper than that," she replied.

In my heart I knew better. The next day while reading my Beth Moore Bible Study, "Believing God to Get to Your Gilgal", I prayed for understanding. Gilgal was the first place the Israelites camped after they crossed the Jordan River into their promised land flowing with milk, honey and grape clusters so large it took two men to carry one cluster. The Israelites set up their 12 memorial stones taken from the middle of the Jordan River to commemorate their place of crisis of decision: whether to return to wandering in the wilderness for another 40 years in unbelief, or cross over in belief to their promised land.

The Lord told Joshua to circumcise all the men to set them apart to be holy and different from their neighbors and to renew His blood covenant with them. At Gilgal, which means circle, God cut away their disgrace resulting from their unbelief. He wounded them so He could heal them and bring them full circle to a new beginning with a new reputation. Now all their enemies feared the children of Israel instead of ridiculing them when they saw God's miracle of drying up the Jordan River.

Jesus similarly consecrated and cleansed me in His blood at salvation, commemorated when we drink juice from the grapes in the Lord's Supper. He has to repeat the circumcision of my heart by painfully cutting away my bondage to idols and strong-holds in order to heal me of my unbelief and keep giving me new beginnings and identities without my previous shame and guilt.

It was no coincidence that He presented me with that circular Winter's Harvest quilt that winter. God was graphically prompting me to break out of my cycle of defeat by believing His Word to enter His promised land of victory.

My Winter's Harvest quilt is my stone of remembrance of God's past miracles during those bleak, barren days when I'm still struggling with the same fears and fleshly desires, and seeing slim breakthroughs as a result of my prayers and labor.

> *"Faith is the substance of things hoped for, the evidence of things not seen" Hebrews.11: 1*

Growing Old Gracefully
as told by Barbara and Doyle Brookshire

Do we all fear growing old, feeble and helpless? I thought so until I heard about 94-year-old Orene Brookshire. She was an independent, spunky entrepreneur until the day she died — doing what she loved most — quilting.

"Nonsense! I can drive over and pay my own rent," she'd tell her son Doyle. "And don't you even dream of taking my car keys again. God has blessed me with good health and two good hands to make quilts. Haven't I been supporting myself with my quilts since my honey died 35 years ago? I can make it on my own just fine, thank you, with a little help from the Almighty.

"Okay Mom, just call if you need me. I love you," Doyle told her, as he hung up the phone in amazement and frustration just two days before Orene went home to be with her Almighty.

Born in 1901 in Tennessee, Orene was one of seven children. She lived frugally through the depression on a farm in Crescent, Oklahoma, raising two children. She was accustomed to hard work, and also sorrow. Her husband died in 1959. She lived alone the last 35 years of her life, never giving up, but occupying her time pursuing her passion — quilting.

Doyle recalls her squealing in delight when she attended one of her last family reunions. Everyone surprised her by dressing in T-shirts created in honor of her. The T-shirts pictured a quilting granny in a rocking chair.

Orene grew old gracefully. She was always seeking opportunities to help others, looking to God for comfort and trusting Him to provide. She never gave up her dreams, nor had regrets because she had the courage to move ahead and tackle whatever God put before her.

> *"They shall still bear fruit in old age." Psalm 92:13-15*

Quilt Stories of

Teaching

The Tic-Tac-Toe Quilt

by Martha E. Rhynes

I gritted my teeth. Last period of the day? Me? Teaching itchy twitchy teenage girls to cook and sew? What had I been thinking? The next day at sixth period, I entered a seldom-used room that housed a few sewing machines and gas stoves. Fifteen girls waited, some resting with their heads on the tables, others reading, some whispering and giggling. They groaned when I announced our first "art" project, a king-size quilt.

"My granny does that quilting stuff with a bunch of old ladies down at the nursing home," said Tina, as she peered into a compact mirror and applied mascara to heavily beaded lashes.

I passed around a list of supplies, which included a shoe box to hold scissors, sewing needles, a spool of white thread, a thimble, and some colorful cotton fabric scraps. The easiest sewing project I could imagine was a Nine Patch coverlet, quilted in a lap hoop in a tic-tac-toe pattern. Since show is always better than tell, I showed them a pieced and quilted Nine Patch square I had made with five 3-inch patterned squares and four alternating white squares. I had quilted the patterned squares in an X figure, and the solid squares in an O figure.

"Perhaps some of you girls have a favorite cotton dress or blouse you've outgrown that you could cut into squares. Fabric in quilts helps us remember important events in our lives. Today, quilt-making has become an art form, but in pioneer times, women made quilts for warmth, as well as for artistic self-expression. On the American frontier, a colorful quilt was often the only object of beauty in a sod house or log cabin. As communities developed, women gathered at quilting bees, where they enjoyed talking and gossiping and singing as they sewed."

Vonnie, a new student, interrupted. "We don't have none of them scraps where I live, and I don't have no dresses to cut up for no quilt." Shunned by the other girls, Vonnie sat in the back of the room with the heels of her cowboy boots on the table and her hands behind her head. Barbed wire tattoos circling well-developed biceps made her an object of gossip. In the teacher's lounge, I'd heard she lived in a foster home after the Department of Human Services removed her from an abusive situation.

"Never mind. I have lots of scraps," I replied. I required each girl to piece and quilt five 9 by 9-inch squares. We needed only 64 squares, but having extras would allow us to select the best ones. When they were finished, I intended to splice the squares together on the sewing machine with strips of fabric. I had bought white cotton material for the strips and backing, and polyester batting for the padding.

The first week, the quilters cut 3 1/2-inch fabric squares. I gave each girl a cardboard pattern and showed them how to pull threads across the grain of the fabric so their squares would be straight, not cut on the bias. They grumbled, "Did you ever hear of anything so dumb? I hate to sew!"

The next week, they surprised me by moving into compatible groups of two or three. They began exchanging fabric scraps — all except Vonnie. She rummaged through my sack of scraps, selected colorful pieces and retired to her corner. I was skeptical that she would produce any finished squares for the quilt.

Most of the girls had never threaded a needle or sewn on a button. At first their stitches were irregular, but each day they improved. As they pieced and quilted, they began chatting about boyfriends, telling jokes, discussing problems with parents, the latest fashion trends, and incidents at school. They forgot I was in the room.

During the third week of quilting, Vonnie came to my desk, "How's this, Miz Rhynes?" She handed me two finished blocks. With an artist's eye for color, she had combined white squares with purple and pink scraps of fabric that I had once used to make a square dance skirt. Her tiny stitches were perfect — 14 to the inch.

"Oh, look, girls!" I said. "Vonnie has made some beautiful blocks for our quilt. Notice how neat her stitches are." I passed them around while Vonnie grinned and looked down at the toes of her cowboy boots.

When I returned the squares to her, she whispered, "My granny taught me how to piece quilts before she died." Soon the girls were competing to see whose stitches were as perfect as Vonnie's. She now sat by Janelle and Kate. During the process of quilting, girls in the class had established a special friendship.

When they finished their squares, I spliced them together with strips of white. Then we sat around a long table and quilted the strips and border in the tic-tac-toe pattern. When the 99-inch square coverlet was finished, we hung it on a wall so students and faculty could see it from the doorway. Everyone admired their handiwork. Mr. Cox, the principal, offered to buy the king-sized coverlet as a gift for his fiancee, so I sold it to him for enough money for future projects. Tina asked, "What project will we start next semester, Mrs. Rhynes? Can we make another quilt?"

"Would you like that?"

Fifteen young quilters shouted, "YES!"

> *"that which we have seen and heard we declare to you, that you also may have fellowship with us; and truly our fellowship is with the Father and with His Son Jesus Christ." 1 John 1:3 NKJ*

Warmth for the Body and Soul

by Donna Barrs

"I'll do the children's sermon," I told my friend, Elaine. She was to be the speaker for United Methodist's Women Sunday. As she shared her thoughts for her first message from a pulpit, I felt the nudge from the Holy Spirit to participate in the service, too. "I don't know what I'll say, but I'm sure God is telling me to do this." With that, my name was printed in the bulletin, and I began the wait, knowing a topic to talk about would be given in time.

Within a week, the words came as I folded a quilt, following a much-needed washing. Still warm from the dryer, my quilt smelled fresh and new, and I found myself looking at it in a way I never had before.

My grandmother made the quilt for me when I was four. Mamaw did a lot of sewing, and this piece was a sight to behold — a colorful labor of love. I don't recall the day I received the gift, but I do remember numerous winter seasons nestled under the patchwork prize.

As the falling of leaves signal the approach of autumn, so the taking down of my quilt marked the arrival of winter. "Sweetie, it's going to be cold tonight," Mother announced. "Let's put the quilt on your bed." Then she removed my carefully folded covering from the top shelf of the closet. As she spread it across my bed, bright swatches of fabric brought sunshine into my room that carried me through the dreary days of winter.

There were a few occasions when my quilt came out of storage during the off-season. I recall picnics with stuffed animal friends, indoor tents, and an upside-down wooden table transformed into a covered wagon with the aid of my quilted canopy. None of these times were as special, though, as the nightly coziness I felt every winter.

The quilt is now faded and less padded, having endured many washings and a little girl's carelessness. No longer a first choice for holding off the cold, it usually remains in the closet when thicker afghans and blankets are selected. I find now, though, that it offers me a special heart warmth.

Closely studying the quilt two weeks before the scheduled children's sermon, I discovered how it reveals some truths that my childhood eyes weren't ready to see. The comfort my quilt gave in my youth is far more reaching now. I compare it to the security provided by God and His church. Knowing I am a part of God's family, and that I have relatives in the spiritual realm to support me on my journey gives me peace that transcends any pain. As a child, I wrapped myself in the quilt. Today, I am enveloped in the love of God's forever family.

My favorite place to read as a child was on my bed. Often when I curled up to enjoy a story, the designs of floral, checked, and solid patches of cloth on Mamaw's masterpiece distracted me. I picked out my favorite colors and shapes, noticing which scraps had also been used to make clothes for my dolls. Now I observe how the pieces stitched together represent those who are drawn as one to form God's church. Different colors and sizes, coming from backgrounds around the world, God's people are diverse. Just as my quilt is held together by stitches, God's children have a common thread binding them — the blood of Jesus Christ.

My quilt bears a unique mark on the bottom corner in bright red. There my grandmother stitched "Donna", giving me an easy way to claim proud ownership. She found a place for my name to crown the fine work of so many sacrificial hours. Again, I see a parallel to God's church. There is a place in it for me — a place etched with my name, perfectly suited for my personality and abilities. Once I was wooed and won over by God's amazing grace, He transported me to a special spot in His kingdom and equipped me to function as a part of His body. Discovering how He has shaped me for use in His work is the single thing that brings me the most excitement and fulfillment.

When my grandmother made the quilt for me, she was rendering a sweet service. Her handiwork was a practical gift that gave me warmth through many long winter nights. My mother's care of the quilt and her consistent use of it for my comfort spoke of her love for me. Now worn and replaced by newer covers, the quilt is kept mainly for sentimental value. However, it represents an unshakable institution of much higher worth. In my heart and mind — the quilt stands for God's church. As my quilt covered and warmed me, the church offers protection and warmth to those in a world cold with sin.

I was next in the order of worship. It was time for the children's sermon, and a group of youngsters approached me. Their faces were so tender and receptive to my words. "Boys and girls, I've brought something special to show you today. This is a quilt my grandmother made for me when I was a little girl. I want to tell you why it reminds me of the church..."

> *"... But how can one be warm alone? Though one may be overpowered by another, two can withstand him. And a threefold cord is not quickly broken."*
> *Ecclesiastes 4:11b-12*

Grandma's Imperfect Sailboat
as told by Mark Wilson

Grandma Wilson made a sailboat quilt for her first of four grandchildren, Mark. However, one of the sails was turned the wrong way. The grandchildren giggled about the mistake, but never dared tell Granny because she was such a perfectionist. It only made them love her more because now they shared a secret that Granny was just like them. They knew they could never live up to her standards — but then, neither could she. They were all flawed.

Mark later confided in his Mom, and she explained, " It's just like God's love for you. You can never earn it by being good enough. He loves you anyway and is always willing to give you a second chance when you confess your sins and shortcomings. As for Granny's imperfect sailboat, she did it on purpose." Mark's mom explained that only God can create perfection. "That was Granny's act of ultimate sacrifice and humility admitting that she wasn't God, and she wasn't perfect. It's called a devil's eye."

> *"For by grace you have been save through faith, and that not of yourselves; it is the gift of God, not of works, lest anyone should boast."* *Ephesians 2:8-9*

Art Lesson

by Betty P. Lyke

My grayish-green college classroom smelled like oil paint and turpentine, tools of students involved in producing art. I, however, was taking Modern Art History. I'd never heard about Mondrian, Pollock or Klee in my southern high school in the 50's. Even Picasso had escaped my scholarship. My goal at that time was to get married and start a family. Now, my babies were almost grown. My new goal was to become a scholar.

When the class began, our professor talked us through various sculptures and colorful paintings projected on a screen. His lecture was exciting, because he was speaking of artists who were still alive. I scribbled furiously in my notebook.

Then, along came Rauschenberg...

I gasped, then hostilely stared at the blown-up slide of a beautiful quilt splashed with buckets of paint. Other students beamed with admiration and approval at what they considered Rauschenberg's "art", but helpless tears came into my eyes.

I instinctively knew the precisely sewn pieces had been carefully chosen from the quilter's box of scraps. I envisioned her digging through the collection, picking up several before discarding them. She chose another, then another, until finally she had the perfect colors with perfect patterns on the fabric. Now, she was ready to piece together the design.

I also knew her thoughts as she worked — thoughts of keeping her family warm during the upcoming winter, especially the children. She thought about her husband and his job that never seemed to pay enough. She thought about supper, and hoped the ground beef would stretch far enough.

The image of my mother's quilting frame hanging from the ceiling when I came home from first grade one day flashed though my mind. "Mama, how did you learn to quilt?"

"Your grandmother taught me," she said with a smile. "You can watch now, while you're little. That's how you start to learn." Her fingers moved skillfully as I stood beside her, sure that I would never be able to create anything quite so beautiful myself. As if she'd read my thoughts she murmured, "When this one is finished, it can be yours."

The professor's distant voice continued with information on artist Rauschenberg as my thoughts went back to the first night with my new quilt on my bed. I sat touching squares that were cut from my old skirts and dresses. I found others that came from my mother's and sister's discarded clothes. I thought about how my grandmother had taught my mother to save, and "make do".

"When you sleep under a new quilt, you'll dream about the boy you're going to marry," Mama had said. I lay awake, picturing all the boys in my classroom, wondering which one it would be. That precious quilt now lay folded on my other grandmother's trunk at the foot of my bed.

The professor noticed my misty eyes and walked over. "This work has really affected you, hasn't it?"

I cleared my throat. "Yes, it has. All I can think about is how much time and thought went into making that quilt. Now, it's ruined."

"But that's the whole point!" he exclaimed. "Don't you see?" I thought about his question. Not wanting to feel ignorant, I took a stab at imagining what the artist was trying to say. Was it to show that although the quilt represented comfort, warmth, and peaceful sleep, there will always be times when those pleasantries will be snatched away by life's harsh reality? Or, perhaps he was saying that the person who knew happiness beneath that beautiful quilt had also experienced coldness and death there as well.

What I did know was that quilts are time-honored symbols of thrift, hard work, and careful planning. Quilts have helped babies go to sleep, and kept old people from getting cold. They have even represented freedom for escaping slaves when they saw them hung as signals on the clotheslines of Abolitionists. These carefully stitched bed covers represent love and warmth in ways few other handmade objects can.

Quilts, without splattered paint, are enduring, magnificent works of art. And that is a lesson I learned before entering Modern Art History class.

Triple Wedding Ring

by Arlene Purcell

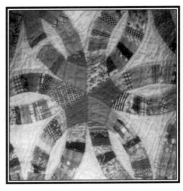

"Tell me the story about Grandad riding horseback in the 1889 Oklahoma Land Run, Mom," five-year-old Arlene begged. "And about Grandmother walking behind the covered wagon all the way from Nebraska with you in her arms." So Fynes Lavern Fleming McGill (1896-1989) patiently wove the fascinating tale once again for her daughter as she tucked her into bed.

Jogged by her daughter's memories, Fynes returned to her quest of finding the elusive Triple Wedding Ring quilt pattern to make a quilt like her neighbor's beautiful wedding quilt. No one seemed to know anything about the pattern, so Fynes took a picture of the actual quilt and mailed it to a magazine with a request for the pattern.

Instead of receiving the pattern, she received 90 requests from other readers for the pattern if she ever found it. Many years later a woman in Nebraska sent the pattern to Fynes. She had almost thrown her mom's pattern away because it didn't make any sense until she saw the picture of the finished quilt in the magazine.

Fynes felt obligated to send the coveted pattern to all 90 readers who'd requested it. She bought extra-large sheets of tracing paper and patiently duplicated the pattern and directions and mailed all 90 copies. As she addressed envelopes and applied the postage, she stopped often to rest and massage her now terribly arthritic fingers.

"I'll never get around to making this quilt at this late date after all the years of searching for the pattern," Fynes sadly told her cousin Fern, visiting from Iowa. "My arthritic fingers won't allow me to quilt anymore."

"I'll be happy to make it for you," Fern said, knowing how much she had her heart set on having that quilt. Nine months later Fern called Fynes. "I've got enough scraps to make a second quilt for Arlene if you'll send me the backing and batting. I'm centering the flowers in each piece. You're going to love it."

"I cherish that quilt today," Arlene said through tears. "You see that was my 30th wedding anniversary gift. We even used it as the backdrop behind the rose trellis in our garden ceremony on the farm when we renewed our wedding vows. The minister explained the significance of exchanging triple vows not only to each other, but also to God who binds us together in His everlasting love. The Triple Wedding Ring is so much stronger than the Double Wedding Ring. When we commit our lives to God first, His perfect love flows through both of us to hold our union together and we become one in Him — true helpmates for life.

"I've always believed that God was in control, but this shows His divine intervention." Arlene continued, "One year after Mom's death in 1989, my sister was visiting the old abandoned home place when the phone rang. It was a woman inquiring if we'd ever found the Triple Wedding Ring pattern we asked for in the magazine 50 years earlier. So I took out more tracing paper and tediously copied the now well-worn pattern and directions once again to mail to her.

"Mom made many new friends corresponding with all the magazine readers who loved this quilt. She felt it her mission to send the requested pattern to each person and also to explain the significance of our loving heavenly Father who is also our husband, and His vital role in making our marriages heavenly. After Dad died, Mom felt secure and cheered in remembering that God was her husband." Arlene concluded with, "It was the healing balm of truth from God's Word that comforted and encouraged her through her grieving."

"For your Maker is your husband." Isaiah 54."

Grandma and I Make a Quilt

by N. Joan Fitzgerald

After Grandma, Mary Alice, had a stroke in 1937 that crippled her left side, her six children decided they would take turns caring for her in their respective homes. I always looked forward to our turn to have Grandma stay with us. She could walk with the help of one crutch, but her left arm hung useless at her side.

One winter when I was about 13 years old, Grandma decided that we should make a Nine Patch quilt. To Grandma, born in 1866, constructing a quilt meant re-cycling stuff on hand. We dug through the scrap box and sorted out any scrap that was big enough to make a 3 1/2-inch square. The least worn parts of outgrown dresses also made good quilt material.

She had made many quilts in her lifetime and had used daintier measurements, but she thought the 3 1/2-inch squares would be easier to manage with only one good hand. She showed me how to make a template of heavy cardboard to place on the cloth. Then Grandma used her crippled left hand to hold the pattern down while she cut out the fabric with her right hand.

Our treadle Singer sewing machine threaded from the left side. Mother moved the machine away from the wall so that Grandma could go around to the back side of the machine to thread it with her right hand.

Grandma cut and sewed together a few squares each day. When I came home from school, I would tear cloth into 3 1/2-inch strips and then cut it into squares. I made more squares in the hour before supper than Grandma had made all day. She would smile and say, "Oh, Joan, you discourage me."

She showed me how the squares should be sewn together with tiny seams. I don't know how she managed it with her one hand because it was hard for me to get the seams narrow and straight using two good hands.

Some of the material was really ugly. I didn't want to put it in the quilt but Grandma said we needed it to make the quilt big enough for my bed. She said we would put it on the bottom where it would tuck under the mattress and no one would see it.

This Nine Patch quilt is my favorite because of the priceless memories it brings me of my grandma. I think of her courage and bulldog tenacity to accomplish her dreams without complaining in spite of her handicap. She was ever my hero, and always lived by the golden rule, "Do unto others as you would have them do unto you."

"*Be strong and of good courage,*" *Joshua 1:6a*

The Flower Garden of Memories

by Marguetta G. Brown

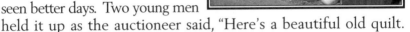

Carelessly slung on a table at the estate auction, the yellowed Flower Garden quilt had clearly seen better days. Two young men held it up as the auctioneer said, "Here's a beautiful old quilt. Who will start the bidding at $20."

Marguetta came alive. Her mother had made that quilt for her sister Correne. The quilt transported her back to the 1930's. " I remember Mother forever carrying around a Sampler chocolate box containing 1 1/2-inch hexagons she had carefully cut," Marguetta said. "Whenever she took a work break with a moment to spare, she'd grab her box and a needle, then she'd start singing that gospel hymn, 'I've got the love and joy and peace of Jesus down in my heart.'

"Joy spread over Mother's face every time she took out a yellow block, representing the sunshine to make the flowers grow." Around the sunshine hexagon Marguetta's mother lovingly hand stitched the floral pieces in which she had centered the calico flower. Then she sewed an outer border of solid hexagons around the floral pieces that were color coordinated to create a harmonious flower garden. When she had completed 60 blocks, she pieced them together with white hexagons.

"Mother's goal was to make a quilt for each of her four daughters," Marguetta explained. "My oldest sister, Myra, said she would rather have a good blanket. Oops, no quilt for her. Although the Flower Garden was mother's favorite pattern, she pieced a Wedding Ring quilt for my second sister, Etta, who lovingly cared for it and later gave it to her daughter, Sally, to treasure. The gift touched Sally's heart but she said, 'Thanks Mom. I love it. But since I don't have anything pink in my bedroom, could you please keep it for me.'"

Twenty years later when Sally returned for her quilt, it had disappeared. Suffering from Alzheimer's, Etta couldn't remember where it was. Sally grieved both the loss of her quilt and her mother's health.

"Mother created identical Flower Garden quilts for Correne and me," Marguetta remembered. " I was so intent on preserving my quilt's beauty, that I carefully rolled and stored it in a pillow case on the linen closet shelf. But Correne cherished her quilt by using it daily to adorn her bed or to wrap herself up in it on chilly nights in front of the fireplace."

"I've got $20. Who will make it $40?" the auctioneer shouted. Marguetta held her card up high and waved rigorously.

Her mind went back to 1945 when her mother searched the county to find a quilter skillful enough to finish her precious creations. Even though $50 was big money in 1945, she was thrilled to pay it for the quality workmanship she received. With admiration in her voice, she pointed to the small, uniform stitches, "There's no better quilting than this. It reminds me of the Garden of Eden, God had a hand in it too." Marguetta's mother taught her girls to cherish and lovingly preserve their quilts.

"I've got $75. Who will give me $100?" the auctioneer's monotone intruded Marguetta's thoughts. *This was insane*, she thought. *That old quilt wasn't worth $20 with all the thread-bare blocks.*

And she remembered a long time ago when her mother worked her needle around those blocks. " I marveled because she was missing an index finger," Marguetta said. "She told me it was because she had extracted a splinter with a pin instead of a needle. She didn't want me to make that same mistake." The finger had become infected and the doctor had to amputate it.

Marguetta frantically waved her card again shouting, "$100." Silence reigned, which seemed to last forever. With the sound of the gavel and the word "Sold," Marguetta burst into tears of joy. The Flower Garden quilt her mother had so lovingly made and given to Correne was now Marguetta's.

"Correne and I were so different," Marguetta explained. "She displayed her quilt, enjoying its beauty until the day she died, while I hoarded and preserved mine." Now that Marguetta owned Correne's quilt, what should she do with it? As she inspected the quilt, she pointed out different blocks to her daughter, Anitra. "This block was made from fabric scraps of a dress Mom made me in fourth grade. And this was from Correne's dress." The quilt was a virtual memory book of all the dresses their mother had stitched for them.

Looking at the quilt in the light of her mother's devotion to her family and God, the quilt took on a patina of love. She had to preserve this quilt. Her daughter-in-law, Kelly, suggested, "I have a friend who restores quilts." Immediately, Marguetta took the quilt to Kelly's friend. The friend returned it clean and bright with the thread-bare blocks replaced. Marguetta's money was well spent.

"I have learned a lesson," she said. " I am enjoying this quilt. It will not sit on a shelf with its beauty hidden. It may be a Flower Garden quilt to others, but to me it is a Garden of Memories — a Garden of Eden." Merely looking at the quilt triggers the memory of that gospel hymn Marguetta's mother sang, and she receives as much joy as her mother did in creating the quilt and as her sister did when she received it and used it. Bless their souls.

"You will show me the path of life; in Your presence is fullness of joy; at your right hand are pleasures forevermore." Psalm 16:11

German Wit and Wisdom

as told by John R. Spillmeier

"John, if I've told you once, I've told you 100 times. Quilt playing with that quilting frame crank!" thundered an exasperated Bertha Beichlein Spillmeier to her small son. "The girls are coming any minute for our quilting bee, and you've messed up the quilt again. Now go outside and play until lunch. Grandmother has been baking your favorite cookies and cake."

John fondly remembers playing under the makeshift tent of the quilting frame with his friends and occasionally helping his grandmother thread her needles. "Those were the good old days," he told his grandchildren as he pulled out his mom and dad's photo album and their all-white wedding quilt with scalloped borders and beautiful quilting in a feather wreath center medallion.

Tears came to his eyes as he read through the album filled with the German wit and wisdom that had been drilled into his head at an early age. Some of the mottos were even penned on some of the Album quilts his mom and grandmother made in Jasper, Indiana. "This is my favorite," John showed his grandchildren as he flipped to the well-worn album page. "It's as pretty as any Hallmark card with the beautifully embellished roses, ribbon and vines. Penned in fancy calligraphy it says:

'Never believe any bad about anybody unless you positively know it to be true.

Never tell even that, unless you feel it to be absolutely necessary.

Remember that God is listening while you say it.'
"Through these beautiful legacy quilts, my German ancestors passed down to you and each succeeding generation their value system of hard work, honesty, kindness and fear of the Lord," John concluded as the grandchildren grew restless.

"You shall teach them diligently to your children and shall talk of them when you sit in your house, walk by the way, when you lie down, and when you rise up." Deuteronomy 6:7

Grandma's Valuable Lessons

as told by Jane Henley

In 1929, five-year-old Jane Henley was angry with her grandma and exploded, "But Grandma, I want to go out and play with everybody else in the new tree house. I don't want to finish hand piecing this silly block — especially if you're going to rip out my stitches and make me do them over like you always do."

Grandma was firm. "Jane, you promised me you would finish your block. I expect you to keep your promise. Remember, we need it to finish your mother's birthday quilt. She's going to love her surprise gift."

Quilting was Grandma's way to keep her granddaughters entertained and out of trouble while they were spending the summer on the Elk City farm. Besides, Grandma believed every young girl should learn to quilt, beginning at the age of four.

Jane obediently finished piecing her block that day and every day. She was rewarded by her surprised mother's praise for her patient accomplishment when the finished quilt was presented at the birthday party.

As an adult, Jane followed her grandma's example. She taught her own daughters and nine granddaughters to piece and quilt at an early age. "It's part of my family heritage and tradition and just as valuable as the legacy quilts I've passed down. Everything that's important, like honesty, hard work, self-discipline, Bible teaching and prayer, must be instilled in children at an early age. Like Grandma's quilting lessons, the tutoring we receive when we're young stays with us to enrich us for a lifetime."

> *"And teach them to your children and your grandchildren . . . " Deuteronomy 4:9b*

One Stitch at a Time

by Delaine Gately

In 1993 I was diagnosed with Chronic Fatigue Syndrome. I felt I could no longer quilt, because I lost the constancy to my stitch and precision was impossible. I almost gave it up until my friend Jean took me to a quilt show.

We examined the beautiful workmanship of each quilt as we strolled down the aisles. Then the graphic color arrangement and visual impact of an antique quilt caught our attention. "What a spectacular work of art!" Jean exclaimed. "But look at these crude stitches. The quilter must have been blind."

"Just when I'd given up all hope of ever quilting again, this woman has inspired me to continue despite my handicap," I excitedly told Jean as I aimed my camera to capture the beauty and my moment of enlightenment. Quilting isn't about perfection. It's about determination and a can-do attitude to complete a quilt that is a gift of love and a testimony of perseverance.

That old quilt changed my outlook. I discarded all my prejudices about doing it "right" and began a new and wonderful journey into quilting. Now they call my quilts "Art quilts". I work in silk and velvets, and the quilts just happen. I'm slow, but steady, and I've found my own style. I truly enjoy finishing a quilt "my way".

I learned an important truth that day — never give up when change comes your way. Be flexible and keep working at it. You'll be amazed what you can accomplish. Quilting, like life, boils down to taking one stitch or one step at a time.

"In God I have put my trust; I will not fear." Psalm 56:4

Quilt Stories of

Giving

The Yo Yo Quilter
by Shanna Lawson

Behind every quilt is the story of the quilter. Seventy-nine-year-old Carolyn shared her story in our counseling session. "At age six I learned from my aunts to quilt, making even, tiny stitches," she said. "But since I became legally blind at age 16, someone has to thread my needles for me." As she reported this memory, she felt for a canvas bag on the back of her wheelchair, and pulled out her calico circles. "If it's alright with you, I'll sew these little Yo Yos together as we talk," she said. "I like to keep my hands busy."

Carolyn was one of my first geriatric patients referred by a psychiatrist for help with depression. Gathering the psychological and social history of patients takes time, but Carolyn's fingers were never still as she told me her past and current problems.

"I was an only child and accepted the Lord at an old fashioned outdoor revival at age 12. I married my next door neighbor at age 14. I love to quilt, sew and crochet. In fact I made this dress I'm wearing many years ago," Carolyn told me as I scribbled down her information.

"Nice work, Carolyn," I complimented her. "Where do you live? And what are your favorite books?"

"I live in a group home for people with disabilities. I love to organize the pot-luck suppers and play the piano for their Sunday evening vespers. My yellow canary, Easter, keeps me company." All this she told me as she stitched red calico circles to yellow ones. "My favorite book is the 'Good Book', the King James Version, of course. My life verse that gives me hope to persevere is, 'They that wait upon the Lord shall renew their strength; they shall mount up with wings like eagles; they shall run and not be weary; they shall walk and not faint.' Isaiah 40:31."

During the two years that Carolyn and I met, I saw her complete three Yo Yo quilts. When I showed interest and told her I also loved to quilt, Carolyn brought a picture album of all the quilts she had completed. She talked about the colors she'd chosen and the methods she used. She explained how she located the fabrics and how she stayed organized. Carolyn's quilts were a source of her positive attitude and an expression of her love for God through creating beauty to give to others. She told me that she sewed each stitch as if she was doing it for Jesus, who had done so much for her. Talking about quilts was healing and became a marvelous metaphor for Carolyn's struggles and successes. This woman had survived overwhelming tragedies —the death of her parents at age 12, abuse of a husband, the Great Depression, loss of an infant at birth, and the burglary of her apartment.

Carolyn always arrived early at my office, via the metro transit van. She was a social person and loved visiting with strangers in the waiting room. One day she overheard my assistant, Sally, ordering flowers for my birthday. She told Sally, "I have the perfect gift for my therapist!" Sally warned me and apologized for letting the information slip.

Normally, therapists are not to accept gifts from clients. But, what if the gift was a multicolored Yo Yo Quilt? This quilt was my favorite. I'd watched Carolyn gather hundreds of circles by hand and attach them to the next Yo Yo, session after session. How could I refuse such a labor of love without damaging the wonderful rapport we had built, I wondered. I had to proceed carefully.

The following week Carolyn came in beaming, "I have a little something for you," she explained. "Every birthday is a gift from the Lord." She reached into her bulging canvas bag and brought out a tiny white package tied with a silk bow. It was much too small to be a Yo Yo Quilt.

I was a bit glad, but sad at the same time. As I opened the package, and the tissue crackled, Carolyn said, "Please, hand me that note."

I handed her the neatly typed Braille note. She read aloud, "This cross is for your Bible, so each day you will know that you have been like an angel to me in my life. I was feeling old and discarded. I pray for you each day that God will continue to guide you as you help others the way you have healed my broken spirit. Even though I am blind, you have helped me see beyond my own limitations. Like my first therapist at the school for the blind when I was a girl, your encouragement to continue quilting has given me hope." My gift was a tiny crocheted red cross. It was so beautiful and touching that I cried.

I still have the Bible marker. Each day as I read my Bible, I wonder if my friend Carolyn is still quilting. Every quilt I see reminds me that not even the loss of sight can prevent us from living a successful and grace-filled life. Even becoming blind at 16 can be turned into a blessing. I have learned many things from being a therapist and a quilter. My Yo Yo quilter's testimony of God's faithfulness strengthened my faith that all things are possible through Him... one day and one quilt at a time.

> *"I can do all things through Christ who strengthens me." Phillipians 4:13*

A Treasured Gift
by Beverly Vokoun

It was April in New Hampshire. Lori Vokoun excitedly ripped open her bridal shower gifts amidst a background of giggles and picture-taking. Finally, just one lone dog-eared package, wrapped in brown butcher paper, remained. It was presented to her with many quizzical expressions. "What could be in this large box?" Lori asked aloud as she examined the postmark from Mustang, Oklahoma, her hometown.

Lori ripped open the paper, then gasped. Tears ran down her cheeks as she gently lifted the gift from its packaging. "It's a handmade Double Wedding Ring quilt from my Mom. She's never made a quilt in her life. I've only been engaged four months, but this must have taken hundreds of hours to make. She must have worked around the clock to finish this gorgeous quilt and get it mailed in time for the shower."

"Look, she enclosed a note."

She began to softly read. "Dear Lori, it was my delight to make this for you. I hope you enjoy having it in your new home. But remember, someday this brand new coverlet will be old and threadbare. Things are not important. Love is. I pray that you and your new husband's love will remain as endless and unbroken as the wedding rings in this quilt. I'm confident it will. Love, Mom."

The whole group of girls was bawling as Lori finished reading. They begged to hear about her mom and Lori's childhood memories.

Tentatively she began, "My dad was killed in a motorcycle accident when I was 12. Mom was left with no insurance, no money, a six-week-old baby, and four other children to support. She did the best she could, but sometimes there wasn't even money to buy food. I ran away with my boyfriend to New Hampshire. When we broke up, I went back to school to get my GED. Then I worked my way through four years of college. Mom was so proud of me.

"She was always there for me, encouraging me, but I was embarrassed because of the way we were forced to live. I'm so ashamed of the way I treated her! Mom is spending all her savings to buy tickets to bring my sisters and brother to the wedding. She's promised to walk me down the aisle.

"And now this! How much hard work and sacrifice it must have taken to make this work of art," Lori whispered.

Tears glistened at Lori's eyes. She smiled. "I'll treasure this forever. One day I'll pass it down to my children. It will be a fitting legacy of my Mother's never-ending, amazing love."

Thanks be to God for His indescribable gift!"
2 Corinthians 9:15

Picture Quilt Worth a Thousand Memories

by Dan R. Olsen

What can a son give his widowed-mother who always says, "I don't need anything for Christmas – so save your money"?

Being an engineer and therefore technical by nature, I decided Mom needed something functional that would also express my heart-felt love. To help spark a creative idea, a friend at work let me borrow one of her home decor catalogs. After extensive perusal, I finally noticed a sofa which was draped with a quilt. Not a typical quilt with flowers or geometric patterns, this quilt was made up of photographs. Mom had just had a hip replacement. I knew then that I would design a pictorial lap quilt to warm her legs and, hopefully, her heart. But where to begin?

Like most engineers, I began at the drawing board. First, I didn't want to be an "inferior decorator" so I needed to pick a background fabric to accentuate her existing furnishings. Secondly, and more enjoyable on a personal level, I needed to find just the right combination of family pictures for the final layout. I also had to find a copier business to transfer the photos on to a high-thread-count fabric for me.

The fun part, from a technical standpoint was arranging the photos in such a way as to maximize the "memories per square foot." God willing, I would be successful in my mission.

Once the design was complete and all of the material collected, I enlisted some experienced help to sew the quilt. I was thrilled with the final product. Now, I just had to wait until the holidays to unveil this once in a lifetime project to my mother.

Christmas Eve finally arrived and I was very excited at the prospect of gift giving.

I asked Mom if her youngest grandson and I could help her open her present. As we lifted the lid and pulled out the quilt I heard her surprised gasp, and she had only seen the back of the quilt at that point.

"There's more Grandma," my son told her, nodding to me as we slowly rotated the quilt so that she could gaze at the family mosaic of quilted frames. She was speechless at first and I could tell she was struggling to hold back her tears of joy.

"I'm overwhelmed... what a priceless treasure!" Mom said between sobs. "Wonders never cease. Who would have thought my left-brained engineer son could create such a artistic expression of his love. Thank you. I'll cherish it forever."

> *"Honor your father and your mother." Exodus 20:12a*

Jennifer's College Quilt
by Lois Pickering

"Oh Mom, we can toss all these old T-shirts," Jennifer volunteered as they were inventorying her clothes for the big move to her dorm room at University of Oklahoma. "I won't be taking them with me to college." So Lois folded all the colorful charity run and event T-shirts Jennifer had accumulated in her years at Putnam City High School and placed them in a plastic bag.

But instead of putting the bag out for the Salvation Army truck the next morning, Lois stashed it in her closet. *I can't bear to throw away all of Jennifer's memories,* Lois thought. *Surely there's something I can do with all these T-shirts.* I know... I'll cut them up and make a quilt for Jennifer to take to college.

So Lois cut and joined the T-shirts together and bordered the quilt top in the school colors of gold and burgundy. Since she didn't have but two weeks to complete it, Lois machine quilted it and finished binding it the night before Jennifer's departure.

As Jennifer unwrapped the mysterious present the next morning, she burst into tears. "Oh Mom, this is so awesome! What a cool surprise. I'm so glad you didn't throw away these T-shirts that bring back soo many memories. I'll cherish my quilt forever and remember you. Thanks for caring so much."

> *"I remember the days of old; I meditate on all Your works;...My soul longs for You like a thirsty land." Psalm 143:5-6*

Dancing Quilts

By M. Carolyn Steele

It was autumn when the thought occurred. The time of storytelling, the Indians would say, when the weather turned cold and everyone wanted to stay warm and trade stories in front of a good fire. Now, however, we adjust the thermostat, and turn on the television. The television – spilling out an assortment of entertainment, usurping the moments when husbands and wives used to share thoughts.

I assumed, at the time, that our recent retirement brought on these observations. But now I am made to think I was bored and lonely. Because, it was then I turned my attention to the ancient trunk that served as a coffee table.

Discovered in the attic, it was hauled down to serve as a toy box. I brightened the dull surface with a coat of yellow paint and peopled the sides with knights and castles sporting flying banners. It held an assortment of toys until our daughters outgrew such things. I claimed the trunk as storage for remnants of fabric when they reached high school and I returned to work as a commercial artist.

"Come here," I called to my husband, Carl, who sat contented with the television's company. "Help me get this glass top off. I want to see what material is in here."

"Are you going to sew something?" he asked.

"No. I just want to see what's inside. Don't you?"

"Not really," he shrugged. But he hefted the large glass slab off the trunk top and onto the carpet. "Must weigh a hundred pounds," he grumbled.

Piles of bright fabric greeted us when we lifted the lid. Hot pinks, oranges, reds, yellows and purples stirred together with strands of glittering sequins.

"Left-over material from all those dance costumes I made for the girls." I fingered a pink knit. "This is from Traci's 'Boogie Woogie Bugle Boy' number. I stamped a million rhinestones on the thing. Remember?"

"What I remember is I thought I'd go crazy if I heard that

song one more time." Carl whistled a few stanzas of the tune whisking us back to the years when our daughters were young and our lives active.

It felt good to recall those busy days. We spent the next hour pulling out shiny satins and knits, trying to recall the dance names each fabric represented. Carl discovered a length of yellow fringe.

"That went with this material." I point to a bright yellow remnant. "It was one of Teri's costumes. The fringe went all down the sleeves."

"Yeah." He frowned. "Wasn't that the picture where she posed like an Egyptian dancer with her hands clasped up over her head? Where are those pictures?"

Where indeed? Stuck in albums, which were stuck in the hall closet. Shut away, just like this material. A piece of red satin shimmered. After all these years, the colors remain vibrant and bold. Scraps of memories. It seemed a shame to throw them away, yet what can you do with scraps?

I like to think it was the material, desperate to be free of the trunk, that whispered the thought — fashion a quilt. One for each girl. A quilt of many colors. I tested the idea.

"What would you think if I made these into quilts for Teri and Traci? We could give them for Christmas."

Carl nodded. "I have an idea. You know how people transfer a picture of themselves onto a T-shirt? Let's hunt up some dance pictures, have them transferred onto white cotton, and surround it with the corresponding fabric."

Ah, I thought, *the material has been whispering to you, too.*

"You're a genius," I said, amazed at his interest.

"Have you ever made a quilt?"

"No. But how hard can it be?"

It didn't take long to realize the folly of my words. We measured and re-measured, deciding on the size and number of squares. Carl designed a grid on the computer and we sat for hours moving the colored squares around.

I was reminded of how much we had enjoyed working together. In the early days, we shared responsibilities on church committees. It had drawn us close and strong in our faith. What happened to us over the years as we worked hard in our respective professions? We drifted away until we became independent of each other.

Carl abandoned the television to flip through albums with me and select photos, reminiscing about each one. The years passed before our eyes as curly-headed little girls became shapely teenagers.

For the first time my husband accompanied me to a fabric store. Together we choose what colors would compliment the dance fabrics. He helped pull the quilt layers taut and stake them with quilting pins on the living room carpet. The whispered idea became a labor of love as the quilts took shape and acquired a certain attitude, youthful and vibrant.

Our daughters were delighted at Christmas with their dancing quilts. Though they didn't know it, their father and I had been given a gift, too. We rediscovered each other's company and a life of shared memories. I wonder, now, why I decided to open a long-closed trunk. Perhaps God chose that moment to touch our souls and remind us of our blessings.

"And my soul shall be joyful in the LORD; It shall rejoice in His salvation." Psalm 35:9

Bitter Sweet Memories

by Jane Rickey

A torrential downpour soaked everything on that dismal morning when they laid my Mother to rest in the family cemetery plot in 1946. But the precipitation didn't equal the tears I shed that day as I begged Dad not to send me and my two-year-old brother, Richard, to Aunt Martha's to live. "Why can't I stay with you and my older brothers? I promise I can take care of myself and won't be any trouble." I begged, but Dad insisted.

That day, not long after my eleventh birthday, I lost not only Mom but also Dad and my older brothers as I was uprooted from my family. I endured the most miserable year of my life. I felt empty and rejected despite the love of my aunt and uncle.

"Oh, Aunt Martha, I could never wear that to Junior High School!" I pleaded a year later about a new dress I was trying on. "It makes me look like a six-year-old. I'd be the laughing stock of the seventh grade."

"You're absolutely right," Aunt Martha agreed. "Maybe we can get the woman who does my alterations to make you a new wardrobe suitable for a mature petite lady like you." So we went shopping for fabric and patterns, and I became the best-dressed seventh grader in Altus, Oklahoma.

I lived with my aunt and uncle until I graduated from high school and then went into nurse's training. I married my handsome doctor on my first job. Two years later when I was expecting my first child, Aunt Martha presented me with a baby quilt. She had taken scraps of the pretty little dresses I had worn throughout junior high and had them quilted for my baby. There was the red and white gingham from my favorite full skirt with the flounce I had worn in the seventh grade... and the lovely black, pink and white stripe from my Sunday dress.

That quilt was such a treasured gift... full of bittersweet memories from my childhood. Each time I see it I thank God for delivering me out of my loss and pain of rejection through the loving care of my aunt and uncle.

A Quilt for my Sister
by Virginia Newton

Following a spate of health and family misfortunes, my sister Sandra was ready to retire as an elementary teacher. More than anything, she wished for a beautiful commemorative quilt to remind her of her long, fruitful career and her many teacher friends.

A consummate organizer, Sandra decided to plan her own "surprise". Swearing me to secrecy, Sandra asked me to choose the pattern, colors, purchase fabric, contact fellow teachers, and create a special retirement quilt for her. Then she clinched the deal by offering to make me a quilt when I retired.

I found an Attic Window pattern to accommodate all the signatures. In October, I cut out blocks of muslin, wrote directions, and mailed 100 blocks. I sent a stack of the six-inch fabric squares and fabric pens to the school counselor.

By January, I had received a few blocks from old friends, but none from the school. I needed all the blocks by February to have time to put them together and hand quilt it for the "Retirement Convocation" for Dallas Independent Schools in May.

Early in February, I learned that the school counselor was out with a broken leg. I called the school and the secretary promised to find the packet and get the teachers to sign the blocks. Several more weeks passed. Finally a package arrived with the cutest blocks. Colorful notes and even a few drawings were written especially to Sandra. "Congratulations on your retirement, Coach!" "Way to go!" and "You deserve the best retirement ever!" These and about 30 other personal memories graced the squares. Now I just hoped I could get it completed in time.

With each stitch, I entreated God to hear my prayers for a longer, healthier life for my sister. I joined the blocks together and created a title block, "Thirty Years on the Playground for DISD." I placed the last stitch in the quilt the day of the ceremony. Sandra loved the quilt. It hung in her house until she died four years later. Making her "surprise" quilt was the last beautiful thing I was fortunate enough to do for my sister.

I never expected to see the retirement quilt Sandra had once promised to make for me. However, the week she died, Sandra enlisted our 92 year old mother to make a red, white, and blue star quilt for my retirement by May so my fellow teachers could sign it. I was one proud lady asking my friends to sign the blocks of the quilt my sister gave me.

Every time I look at my quilt, I remember that even as Sandra was leaving this life, she wanted to provide a quilt for her sister.

" . . . whatever you want men to do to you, do also to them . . ."
Matthew 7:12 NKJ

The Prophetic Quilt

by Irene Ruth Rennhack,
Director of the American Museum of Quilts

I remember watching grandmother, Florence Kuder, cut endless patches from our outgrown clothes as we huddled around the pot-bellied stove on cold winter nights. Using a quilting frame set up on the sun porch of our home in Allentown, Pennsylvania, she taught me how to quilt. Occasionally I went with her to quilting bees at the Ladies Aid Society meetings at her church in Macungie, Pennsylvania. When I moved to California after my marriage and got involved with the Santa Clara Valley Quilt Association, my real love for quilts surfaced.

Mother flew out to California one Christmas, gingerly cradling a mysterious package in her arms.

"What in the world is this?" I asked as I relieved her of her awkward burden.

"That's your 'Prophetic Quilt' from grandmother Kuder," Mother said as she climbed into the car. Curiosity propelled me to rip open the package and carefully unfold the most beautiful red and white Irish Chain quilt I'd ever seen. The workmanship was exquisite, and in the corner a paper tag was pinned that read: "This quilt is for Irene, from Grandmother Florence Kuder, 1906."

Seeing the puzzled look on my face, Mother explained, "In early 1906, Florence and her sister, Hannah, were working on this quilt together when Hannah caught the influenza. Florence nursed her night and day. Hannah told her not to grieve if she died, because before the year was out, God would comfort her by giving Florence a little girl to take care of.

"Hannah died in February and I was born 11 months later on December 29, 1906, just as she had prophesied," Mother concluded. "Your grandmother wished to pass along to you the same comfort and blessings she received from God while she was finishing your Prophetic Quilt."

"Your eyes saw my substance, being yet unformed. And in Your book they all were written, the days fashioned for me, when as yet there were none of them." Psalm 139:16 NKJ

The Healing Hands Quilt

by Sharon Newman
Quilt Author, Lecturer and Appraiser

Among my many trips was one to a quilt guild in Los Alamos, New Mexico to do a lecture and workshop. I filled my suitcase with many quilts and some of the fabrics from my reproduction line. The guild loved the workshop and the lecture and bought my fabrics. The ladies found out that I might require another treatment for a cancer discovered in 1993 while writing some quilt books.

Several months later, the guild gifted me with a quilt containing many of the fabrics I had sent them. The blocks are star patterns called Eddystone Light. The design has eight pointed stars in 14 blocks, set in a symmetrical arrangement with four blocks across and seven down. The four corners have extra background blocks. In red thread, the women quilted healing hands all over the quilt.

My Eddystone Light quilt with lots of cheerful red prints brightens my dreary days since losing my husband and battling cancer. It provides me with hope and light to find the way in my darkest hours.

The label is outlined with red hearts and has the names of the precious ladies who worked on it: Maryann Allison, Mary Norris, Teri Devine, Kathy Gillespie, Sue Friar, Lynn Provost, Jan Warren, and Christy Maning as a reminder of their love and prayers.

Three years later, I took my Healing Hands quilt to Houston to lift my spirits when I had a new treatment for cancer. The doctors and nurses were fascinated that so many women cared enough to make such a beautiful token of their love.

I am currently free of cancer, and daily praise the Lord for His healing strength and for the sacrificial love demonstrated by Maryann, Mary, Teri, Kathy, Sue, Lynn, Jan and Christy in my Healing Hands quilt, stitched to comfort and console me during my times of greatest need.

Quilt Stories of

Helping

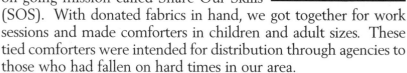

Sam and the Magical Comfort

by Muriel Pech Owen

A few years ago, when there was so much talk of the homeless problem in our country, our quilt guild decided to do what they could to help ease a little of the problem.

That winter, we began what is now an on-going mission called Share Our Skills (SOS). With donated fabrics in hand, we got together for work sessions and made comforters in children and adult sizes. These tied comforters were intended for distribution through agencies to those who had fallen on hard times in our area.

The quilting ladies generously responded to our idea with warm hearts and eager fingers. From the beginning, the pile of fluffy, colorful children's quilts quickly grew into a mountain. We contacted the local YWCA for our first distribution to find out when we might deliver our offerings to them. We asked if we might call in the local newspaper and make it a photo opportunity to encourage others to help the homeless in their own way.

On the designated day, we arrived at the YWCA and unloaded our cars and vans, piling row upon row of happy, warm, colorful quilts on long tables in a big room. The stacks reached to our chins as we busily worked to get them all out and ready to be "adopted."

I asked the YWCA staff if they had a parent and child who might be willing to have their pictures taken by the news media. After a short conference, the door opened and a mother came into the room with a young boy of about four years of age. Shyly, the boy hid behind his mother's legs and looked about. I watched as we moved stacks of comforters about. Curiosity caused the child's fingers to reach out and squeeze a corner of a quilt. He smiled.

Cautiously, I approached him and settled down on my haunches to have an eye-to-eye chat.

I asked his name. "Sam," he replied.

"Well, Sam, what if I told you that you can have any quilt

from any stack in this room. What would you say?"

Sam studied me and said nothing.

Another of our quilt ladies approached and unfolded a pleasant child's comforter about 45 inch x 60 inch that had airplanes and cars and trucks on it. "Sam, do you like this one?" He nodded.

"Or do you like this one better?" She opened a red, yellow and blue creation. Sam backed up behind his mother and studied both comforters silently.

Sam's mother bent and whispered something in his ear. Then, he grinned and stepped forward toward my friend. I watched her open several comforters and Sam inspected them gravely.

Finally, Sam selected a bright masterpiece with royal blue borders. He took it and wrapped it about his little body and laughed. Such a beautiful laugh. His entire face shone with his delight.

For the next several minutes, Sam flew about the room as Superman might with his "comforter-cape" about his shoulders. Then, Sam was under the table, hiding beneath his "comforter-tent," singing to himself.

Suddenly, Sam was once again beside his mother, tears streaming down his face as he handed his newfound treasure back to his mother. I was close enough to hear his words.

"But, Mama, we don't have any money to pay for this."

My heart broke. Obviously, this young man had heard those words over and over as life had denied him his heart's desire. Today, I was able to bend down to a young Sam and explain that this was our "gift" to him and there was no price to pay. We wanted Sam to have the comforter; we had made it especially for him.

He studied me for a moment, then smiled a sparkling smile, and looked up at his mother, who nodded. In the next instant he clutched his bounty to him, then whipped it about his shoulders and once again flew about the room, completely carefree in his own happy, magical, child-world.

I'd planned to bring this child a quilt, but Sam had given me a gift.

"It is more blessed to give than to receive." Acts 20:35

SOS, East Bay Heritage Quilters; DeAnna Davis, 210 Crocker Ave, Piedmont, CA 94610

Quilting to Survive - Ugly Quilts

by Eleanor Dugan

As she rode toward San Francisco's glittering Symphony Hall, Francette Martin's mind was on an evening of Mozart. But suddenly, she grabbed her husband's arm.

"Stop!" she shouted.

He hit the brakes hard, fearing they'd struck something. As irate horns blared behind them, Francette pointed to a man sleeping in a doorway.

"See that plaid sleeping bag?" she asked proudly. "I made it!"

Most of us have seen men, women, and even children living on the street and felt helpless to do anything. No one of us alone can solve the staggering economic and social problems behind this urban tragedy. We instinctively avert our eyes and turn our minds to more positive thoughts.

My Brother's Keeper (MBK) quilters are keenly aware of this constant social paradox — of desperate need in the midst of our society's traditional plenty. But instead of turning away, members of this organization use their needles to alleviate some of the suffering. They are busy turning 100% recycled materials into emergency sleeping bags.

The first sleeping bag was made in 1985. Flo Wheatley, a nurse in Hopbottom, Pennsylvania, designed it on her kitchen table. Her neighbors soon offered to help. Since then, MBK has become a national grassroots movement, with individuals and groups making and distributing more than 100,000 free emergency sleeping bags to people on the street. The bags are basically large, tied comforters, folded and sewn into big pillowcase carriers.

Our predecessors sometimes filled their bed covers with leaves, cornhusks, newspapers, or pine needles for warmth. These modern survival units use old clothes, leftover church rummage, and torn blankets and mattress pads.

Some quilters don't make the connection between the visceral aspects of this work and the history of American quilts and quilting. Founder Flo Wheatley even warns new organizers that, "Real quilters rarely want to do this. They think it's beneath them." In fact, Flo found so many potential volunteers who were frightened by the very word "quilt" ("Oh, I could never sew well enough to make a quilt!") that she nicknamed the bags "ugly quilts". This deprecating qualifier has reassured and liberated hundreds of timid seamstresses who might not otherwise have participated.

But in San Francisco, some 'real' quilters have taken up the project. They've found that the survival aspect of assembling anything at hand into emergency covers offers a powerful spiritual link to our foremothers. The bags are strictly utilitarian, fashioned quickly from clean discards to provide essential warmth, yet each quilter somehow incorporates her own vision and creativity as she chooses among the available materials.

"Ugly" these bags rarely are, and the warmth they impart to the user is echoed in the heart of the maker. There is an upbeat, almost embarrassingly emotional fulfillment in realizing that the work of your hands can literally save a life.

As one volunteer puts it, "I think of it like gardening. A lot of folks would rather arrange flowers in a vase than shovel manure. Well, this is 'shoveling,' but it's equally satisfying on a very fundamental level."

The project is not without critics. Some oppose it, feeling that sleeping bags are insulting "bandaids" for people who desperately need and deserve so much more. Others warn, "You're just encouraging them."

"Yes," responds San Francisco volunteer Becky Gordon. "I am encouraging them — encouraging them not to die. I don't personally have the power to solve the overwhelming economic and social problems that have put 10,000 homeless people on the streets of my city, but I can make it possible for some of them to survive one more night until things can change in their lives. And I'm doing it with my quilting skills. I feel very close to my quilting ancestors when I do this."

> "If a brother or sister is naked and destitute of daily food, and one of you says to them, 'Depart in peace, be warmed and filled,' but you do not give them the things which are needed for the body, what does it profit?" James 2:16

My Brother's Keeper Quilt Project,
Flo Wheatley, RR1, Box 1049, Hopbottom, PA 18824, 570-289-4335, mbkqg@epix.net, www.uglyquilts.org.

Quilting for the Lord

by Kay Gibson

"Next, we have a stunning Rail Fence quilt, nicknamed "The Watermelon Patch" in honor of our hometown twins, Big and Little Holmes, who have sold watermelons all their lives," Willie, the enthusiastic auctioneer announced. "Step on up folks and look at this beautiful handmade work of art created by our Watson Quilters, right here in Watson, Missouri, population 321. Remember, all proceeds go to Dick who has Lou Gehrig's disease. Along with mounting unpaid medical bills, Dick and his wife still have children in school to feed and clothe.

"Who will start the bidding at $400?... Yep, I've got $400... Ok, now $450?... I see $450... Who will make it $500?... I've got $500... Do I hear $550?... Going once... going twice... sold to bidder number 58 for $500," Willie yells triumphantly.

"That concludes the auction, folks. The total raised for Dick and his family including the $1500 for quilt raffle tickets was $9858. We couldn't do it without your generosity. Dick and his wife thank each of you who bought and sold raffle tickets, donated food, auction items, and the Watson Quilters who quilt for the Lord."

We love quilting for the Lord. Occasionally we make quilts for ourselves. But if an emergency auction comes up, we pull some of our own quilts out of storage and auction them. As the Bible says, it is more blessed to give than to receive.

> *"Let your light so shine before men, that they may see your good words and glorify your Father in heaven." Matthew 5:16 NKJ*

United We Stand, Divided We Fall

as told by Frances Thompson

Frances Thompson was gasping for air with pain shooting through her chest when she awakened her husband, Wes. He hurriedly dressed and threw a robe around Frances before rushing her to the hospital. After extensive waiting and testing, the Doctor scheduled surgery the next morning to replace her mitro valve the second time.

Marge Thompson and Dorothy Catledge, friends from the Lexington United Methodist Church where Wes was interim pastor, brought Frances flowers and a beautifully wrapped gift a few days later. "We wanted to bring you something to make your recovery time fly by," explained Dorothy as Frances opened the package to discover a fat bundle of cheerfully colored calico diamonds. "There are 277 diamonds we cut out for you to piece together to make a Lone Star quilt for your daughter Sarah's birthday," Marge added. "We'll sit and piece with you to keep you company if you'd like."

"But I've worked all my life teaching school and never had time for needlework," Frances objected. "This is so overwhelming! I wouldn't know where to begin or what to do."

"We'll teach you. It will be great fun!" both ladies chimed in. "With both of us helping, we'll complete the top by the time you're on your feet again."

The ten days Frances was in the hospital and the additional 30 days of recovery at home went quickly. She loved her new pastime of making a quilt and visiting with friends. "Do you think we'll finish the top before Wes and I leave for our new church in November?" Frances asked.

"Not at this rate, we won't. I know, let's have a sewing party and invite all the women at church to meet in fellowship hall next Monday morning. We'll all bring potluck lunches and whip it out in no time. It will be your going-away gift from all of us to you," Dorothy volunteered.

By 4:00 p.m. the following Monday, the United Methodist ladies of Lexington had finished the beautiful Lone Star quilt top, complete with borders to make it large enough for a king-size bed. Frances was elated when they presented it to her — a true united labor of love and symbol of their deep affection and care for her while she was recuperating. She cherished the memories made learning to sew with these dear friends.

Wes's announcement that the quilt top had been lost in the move was a tragic blow to Frances. "Oh no!" she sobbed. "That was my very first quilting project. After I showed it to Sarah, she couldn't wait to display it on her bed."

"Don't cry," Wes consoled her. "I'll cut out 277 more calico diamonds and you can start all over again. The church ladies here will be happy to help you. It will be a great way to get acquainted and a beneficial learning experience to perfect your sewing skills."

The second time was a charm. The Lone Star top was completed and sent three months later to be quilted by their old church friends in Garber where Wes had also pastored. It was finished just in time for Sarah's birthday.

Sarah still proudly displays it on her bed ten years later and never tires of sharing the story of her twice-created quilt made by all their friends in three different United Methodist Women's Groups where Wes had served.

"Behold, how good and how pleasant it is for brethren to dwell together in unity!" Psalm 133:1 NKJ

Promise Quilts

By Mary Greeno

In 1995 I had a routine mammogram and heard those dreaded words, "You have breast cancer." While I was hospitalized for a total abdominal hysterectomy, they did the breast biopsy. It seemed unbelievable that I would have to return to the hospital just five weeks after the hysterectomy to have a mastectomy. However, even then, I considered myself lucky to have found the cancer when the lesion was only the size of a grain of sand.

As the saying goes, "When life gives you scraps, make quilts." While I recuperated from the two surgeries, my self-prescribed therapy was to make two blocks per day for my "Find Your Favorite Plaid" scrap quilt. Each day when my husband came home from work, I proudly showed him what I had accomplished. Some might see the quilt as a reminder of a difficult time in my life. I see it and say, "I faced cancer and survived."

In 1997, local TV news co-anchor, Chrys Peterson, honorary chairperson of the Northwest Ohio Komen Race for the Cure© interviewed me and discussed how quilting had been therapeutic during my recuperation. At the end of the interview, she asked if I could donate a quilt to the local Race for the Cure©. I was not familiar with Race for the Cure©, but that was about to change.

The TV interview was in March and the Race was in September. Just six months to create a quilt meant that I had to enlist the help of my close quilting friends. We chose a two-tone Snail's Trail pattern in pale pink and cream, and named it Pink Promise. Pink is for breast cancer awareness and Promise just seemed fitting. Raffle tickets totaling $2200 were sold for the quilt. Breast cancer survivor, Gwen Gregory, proudly claimed the quilt with her winning ticket. Gwen is saving the quilt as a wedding gift for her daughter. In the meantime, whenever Gwen feels blue, she finds comfort by wrapping herself in the quilt.

Fast forward to 2004. We have just raffled the seventh Promise

Quilt, Heartfelt Promise, which raised $27,058. Much has happened over the past few years. This core group of quilters has become known as the Promise Quilters because we promise to make a quilt every year until a cure is found for breast cancer. Each quilt has "promise" in its name. Breast cancer survivors have claimed the winning ticket to three of the seven quilts.

The quilts are created in my sewing room, a.k.a. "The Sylvania Sweatshop" where as many as ten quilters work assembly-line fashion. Many of these women, all with families, responsibilities and busy lives, have told me that it is an honor to be included in the group. The group always includes a significant number of breast cancer survivors; in fact, we may soon reach the point where each quilt is made entirely by breast cancer survivors. To date we have raised over $95,500 for the Northwest Ohio Affiliate of the Susan G. Komen Breast Cancer Foundation.

Each quilt has its special memory. Pink Promise was like raising a first child with many lessons learned. A recently diagnosed woman happily claimed the Paisley Promise. She said the quilt had "made her year." A nun bought the winning ticket for Pineapple Promise. She re-raffled it to benefit her favorite charity. A survivor won the Album Promise and carried it with her as she dealt with the emotional and physical trauma of moving her mother into a nursing home. The six o'clock news captured the delivery of the Perennial Promise. Anniversary Promise commemorated the twentieth anniversary of the national Race for the Cure© and the tenth anniversary of the Northwest Ohio Race for the Cure©. The pattern for Heartfelt Promise was donated by Kathy Love of Love Quilt Patterns, whose sister was undergoing treatment for recurrent breast cancer. The hand embroidery on the quilt was done by my mother, who died six months later. My dear quilting friends purchased a companion pillow at a silent auction so that I would have a piece representing my mother's last project.

The Promise Quilts can best be described by the label on Pink Promise: "Making a quilt, like planting a tree, is an act of love and faith in the future." I marvel at the Promise Quilters' accomplishments, not just because of the money raised from the quilt raffles but because of their commitment to fighting breast cancer, a disease which, statistically, will hit one in every eight women. Creating a Promise Quilt enables us as survivors to strike back at a disease so that someone in the future can live.

Peggy's Angels Network
by Susan Loyacano

"I know... we could call ourselves Peggy's Angels," DyAnna volunteered from the back seat as they traveled to the Oklahoma Quilters Retreat. "We could perpetuate Peggy's dreams to make quilts for the babies in the neo-natal ICU and raise money for the Senior Center. Can you believe the last quilt we made with Peggy brought $1600 for the Seniors?"

The foursome had been inseparable — quilting, shopping, traveling and celebrating life together. But now, mourning the death of Peggy, their ringleader, they were desperate to keep alive her vision of quilting to help others. Their first project was to complete all of Peggy's UFOs — unfinished objects.

In June of 2001, they held a "Round Robin" sewing day and completed 32 quilt tops with lots of help from other quilters. Fabric stores, as well as individuals generously donated material, batting and thread. Local quilt shops helped Peggy's Angels by machine quilting the tops.

In a few short years, Peggy's Angels has donated over 130 quilts to local nursing homes, battered women's shelters, homes for young mothers, children with life threatening illnesses, cancer patients, mothers and babies at risk. Peggy's Angels' scrapbook is filled with thank you notes and photos of the quilt recipients. "Don't you know Peggy is smiling down on us," Susan said to her quilting buddies as they added new photos to the album and wiped away tears. "It's so rewarding to carry on Peggy's dreams of sharing love with others and to memorialize her through each quilt."

"And let us not grow weary while doing good, for in due season we shall reap if we do not lose heart."
Galatians 6:9

From Rags to Riches

by Carla Burt

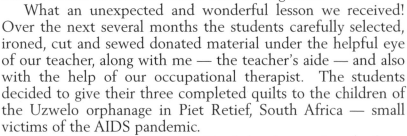

It began as a sewing lesson for our small class of Life Skills students in the fall of 2002. Our lead teacher, an experienced quilter, decided that having each child make a quilt for someone less fortunate could teach more than sewing skills.

What an unexpected and wonderful lesson we received! Over the next several months the students carefully selected, ironed, cut and sewed donated material under the helpful eye of our teacher, along with me — the teacher's aide — and also with the help of our occupational therapist. The students decided to give their three completed quilts to the children of the Uzwelo orphanage in Piet Retief, South Africa — small victims of the AIDS pandemic.

A local newspaper reporter visited the class to view the fruits of their labors. The story and photo of the students and the quilts appeared in our local newspaper. Then the project began to snowball. I received telephone calls from people whose hearts are easily touched by the hurts and needs of others: "Could I please make a quilt for the children?" "Our youth group would like to make quilts for the orphans." "I've never quilted, but my friend is willing to help me. May I donate a quilt?"

For me it was a humbling experience to see the outpouring of love and concern.

In June of 2003 I packed up 15 quilts and headed to Africa to be with my daughter for the birth of her first child. Miraculously, that number of quilts exactly matched the number of children and caregivers living at Uzwelo. In Africa most people live on the edge of survival. Blankets are treasured possessions, often used as backpacks to carry children and later to provide warmth for them against the freezing nights.

Arriving at Uzwelo ("Mercy" in Zulu), we displayed these colorful gifts of love on a fence. Africans love color. One by one, beginning with the house mothers and down to two-year-old Boetie ("little brother") each member of the Uzwelo family chose his favorite quilt. Each child, black eyes wide with awe, waited patiently for his turn to lovingly pick out and then to touch his quilt. Joy lit every face as they gently lifted their quilts off the fence. The hugs, tears, smiles and repeated "Thank you, Thank you" were unspeakably endearing as recipients delightedly wrapped their quilts around them. The drab yard danced as if filled with beautifully colored butterflies.

Out of one person's cast-off rags emerged precious riches, sent with love to bless and enrich the lives of others, unseen, unmet, yet cared for and valued just the same. One small act of kindness by three young handicapped children blossomed into blessings for many, many more, both givers and receivers alike.

More quilts have been made and sent by the youth group at All Saints Parish in Peterboro, NH. Funds raised by youth groups from New Hampshire, Massachusetts and California have enabled Wellspring Ministries in Piet Retief to purchase a food freezer and begin a weekly food program for mothers and children who used to forage daily at the local dump.

"Show Me your faith without your works, and I will show you My faith by My works" James 2:18b

Yes, There is a Santa

by Carol Babbitt

In October, 1998, I heard about Project Linus, which is a nonprofit organization that makes and distributes handmade blankets and quilts to children in need. My children were finally in school all day, and I was ready to fulfill the second part of my life's dream. I didn't dream about stardom, fame, or even riches. From the time of my earliest memory, I dreamt of two things: I wanted to be a mother, and I wanted to help others.

My aspirations of motherhood came from watching my own mother. I wanted to be just like her — glamorous, smart and loving. Since she had lots of babies, I spent hours pretending I was her, caring for my baby dolls.

When I was six, I learned about helping others through a Sunday school service project. Our teacher gathered our class together like a mama duck with her baby ducklings and led us across the street to the home of an elderly woman to present her with a fruit basket. I cannot describe the dramatic impact that one small act of kindness had on my life and my future. From that time on, I wanted to have that warm-fuzzy feeling non-stop that comes from helping others.

I knew immediately that Project Linus was right for me. I loved to quilt and sew. Bringing a little comfort to children by doing something that I found so enjoyable was the perfect fit. I began making blankets for my local chapter in Bloomington, Illinois. In October of 2000, I was elected President of the national organization. I can truly say that my dreams have come true. I have a wonderful husband, beautiful children, and I volunteer my remaining time to an organization that I love.

From time to time Project Linus is blessed to receive notes from those children and their parents who have received blankets. One special note came recently from Susan, the mother of two small children, four-year-old Heather and Joshua, 14 months old. Joshua was born prematurely and spent time in the NICU at the local hospital where he received his Project Linus blanket.

The blanket accompanied Joshua during 18 hospital stays. In November he had a complete airway reconstruction. As always, the nurse placed his blanket in his crib during the surgery. Unfortunately, when they returned Joshua to his bed after the surgery, the blanket had mysteriously disappeared. The entire family was crushed.

As Christmas approached, Susan took Heather to visit Santa. When asked what she wanted for Christmas, Heather told Santa the only thing she wanted was to have her baby brother's blanket back. Susan tearfully pondered what to do. She couldn't make such a gift herself. Out of desperation, she contacted her local Project Linus Chapter Coordinator who joyfully agreed to send a new blanket. In the words of a very grateful mother, Susan said, "Project Linus saved our Christmas Day! My daughter will continue to believe in Santa, and my little son will have another special blanket for his next trip to the hospital. Thank you from the bottom of my heart. You have blessed us twofold."

"We know that the children are the reason we devote our time to Project Linus," Carol said speaking for her fellow volunteer quilters. "The reward of bringing those precious little ones the tiniest amount of comfort is enough. But in our hearts we really know that we receive the greatest gift in the giving."

"Give, and it will be given to you; good measure, pressed down, shaken together, and running over..." Luke 6:38

www.projectlinus.org, Information@projectlinus.org, P.O. Box 5621 Bloomington, Ill 61701-5621

How to Help

Project Linus, P.O. Box 5621, Bloomington, IL 61702-5621, 309-664-7814; www.projectlinus.org; project.linus@verizon.net

Wrap Them in Love, 401 N. Olympic Ave., Arlington, WA 98223; 360-435-4949; www.wraptheminlove.org

Newborns In Need, P.O. Box 385, Houston, MO 65483; 417-967-9441; www.newbornsinneed.org

ABC Quilts (At-risk Babies Crib Quilts), 569 First NH Turnpike, Northwood, NH 03261; 603-942-9211; www.abcquilts.org

Kids 'N Kamp, 3440 Olentangy River Rd., Columbus, OH 43202; 614-262-2220; www.kidsnkamp.org; KNKamp@aol.com

Once Upon a Quilt Co., 3404 Griffin Rd., Ft. Lauderdale, FL 33312; 954-987-8827; www.onceuponaquilt.com; OUAQ@aol.com

Binky Patrol, Inc., P.O. Box 1468, Laguna Beach, CA 92652-1468; www.binkypatrol.org; binky@binkypatrol.org

SOS (Share Our Skills to Comfort Others), East Iowa Heirloom Quilters, P.O. Box 1382 Cedar Rapids, IA 52406-1382

Children's Quilts, East Bay Heritage Quilters; DeAnna Davis, 210 Crocker Ave, Piedmont, Ca 94610

My Brother's Keeper, Flo Wheatley, RR 1, Box 1049, Hopbottom, PA 18824, 570-289-4335, mbkqg@epix.net, www.UGLYQUILTS.ORG

Promise Quilters for Susan B. Koman Race for the Cure; Mary Greeno, 419-841-8867, 30 Woodforest Parkway, Sylvania, OH 43560, promisequilts@toast.net

Quilts for Injured Soldier, Quilters Guild of Southern Maryland, www.qgsm.org, RB395@aol.com

Also Check Your Local Quilt Guild for Opportunities to Help

Editors & Contributors

Lisa Alexander lives in The Colony, TX, with four children — a toddler, a ten-year-old and two teenagers. She has written for *The Dallas Morning News*, *Dallas Child* and *Writer's Digest*, and is Communications Coordinator of a downtown Dallas church.

Donna Barrs writes from her home in Montgomery, AL, where she lives with her husband and two sons. A childhood in the South, a 24-year teaching career, and a calling to write for God's glory are the inspirations for her poems, devotionals, and short stories.

Martha Baxley is a product of the Great Depression, an Oklahoman and proud of it. After a life as a rancher's wife and elementary teacher, she loves writing, public speaking, and square dancing. Martha has two daughters and four grandchildren.

Shirley J. Bergman was raised in MI. An elementary teacher in Utica, MI, before retiring in 2000, Shirley has been published in *Marguette Monthly* and *Michigan History Magazine*. She enjoys anything to do with history, genealogy, and the Arts.

Kay Bishop, M.Ed., a former magazine editor, columnist, writer and teacher conducts creativity workshops.

Mary Brelsford, bride of Joe J. Brelsford, U.S. Navy, W.W.II, 1942, is a graduate of Texas Christian University, Fort Worth, TX, B.A. Journalism, wife, mother, grandmother, great-grandmother, quilt maker and longtime member of Trinity Valley Quilter's Guild,

Elaine Britt is a wife, mother, writer, speaker, and full-time Interior Decorator. She is a contributing author to Cup of Comfort Devotionals, and But Lord, I was Happy Shallow by Marita Littauer, and various Christian magazines.

Velda Brotherton writes a weekly newspaper column in Winslow, AK where she was born and lives with her husband. She has written six Western Historical novels and three non-fiction books. Her short stories are in two anthologies. www.authorsden.com/velda.

Marquetta Griswold Brown is a retired teacher and a former Assistant Editor in the Home Department of *The Progressive Farmer* magazine. She and her husband, Graydon, have four children and four grandchildren.

Carla Burt is the mother of three, grandmother of two with two on the way. Carla worked as a Special Ed Teacher Associate for 19 years. She loves the Lord, to read, do handcrafts and be with her family and Carl, her hero and husband of 32 wonderful years.

Carol Cutler wrote a book about God's care for her. A teaching leader for Bible Study Fellowship in Oklahoma City for 16 years and leader for 12 years of Women's Ministry in her church, she loves photography and creating greeting cards called From My Garden.

Holly Doyle resides in Marlton, NJ. She enjoys sewing, quilting, paper crafts, and being an entrepreneur. She is inspired by nature and all the wondrous things God has created for us, reusing and recycling whenever possible.

Eleanor Dugan is a San Francisco based writer-editor, a quilter, and a ten-year volunteer with My Brother's Keeper Sleeping Bag Project. For info on MBK, send a SASE to Flo Wheatley, RR 1, Box 1049, Hopbottom, PA 18824 or phone 570-289-4335 or email mbkqg@epix.net. Visit their Website @ WWW.UGLYQUILTS.ORG.

Helen Upton Earhart, born in Middletown, OH, moved to CA in 1956. She took quilting lessons at Grossmont College, La Mesa, then started teaching in Rogue River, OR. Helen is working on her 91st quilt and has taught over 200 quilters.

Delaine Gately's love of quilts started during childhood naps. She collects old quilts, believing she's their guardian and they are gifts of love and determination. She belongs to two guilds, a quilt circle and is a support group leader for Fibromyalgia.

Mary Greeno and her husband Duane live in Sylvania, OH. Since being diagnosed with breast cancer in 1995, Mary has established the Promise Quilters and the Heart-in-Hand Quilters. She is an American Cancer Society's Reach-to-Recovery volunteer. 410-941-9978, promisequilts@toast.net.

Frederica Griffith is a teacher, editor, lecturer and a member of the American Association of Christian Counselors. She and her husband, Carvason, have three adult children, whom they home-schooled.

Nancy Harris is a happy wife, mother and grandmother in Norman, OK. She facilitates a weekly Ladies Bible Study, runs around with a madcap group of ladies in the Red Hat Society, attends OU basketball games and spoils her grandchildren.

Melanie Hemry is an award winning writer and winner of the coveted Guideposts Writing Contest. She has hundreds of published articles to her credit and has ghostwritten ten books, two of which won Angel Awards.

Lynne Herbert lives in Thunder Bay, Ontario, north of Lake Superior. When the winters turn cold, and the landscape is white with snow, it seems natural to sew rosy quilts to snuggle in.

Shanna Chechovsky Lawson, LCSW is a psychotherapist in Oklahoma City. She has been writing and teaching about life and spirituality for 20 years. She is working on a creative non-fiction book about how God has healed her and the lives of her patients.

Tricia Lehman is a mother of five and the delighted grandmother of two. She is a professional machine quilter who also loves to write.

Susan Loyacano was born in Ypsilanti, MI, and lives in Kansas with her husband of 31 years, Mark. Susan is an Accounting Manager for an insurance agency and spends time with her son Anthony, Regina, and her three grandchildren.

Betty P. Lyke has sold to numerous publications for children and adults: *Grit, Today's Christian Woman, Radar, Texas Gardener, Living with Teenagers.* She wrote a column for Home Cooking for 13 years, and now a weekly gardening column for The Paris News.

Marsha Mueller has professional experience in writing and publishing, particularly in the medical and healthcare areas. She also has experience in design and graphic arts, and in public relations and advertising.

Chalise Miner writes for magazines and newspapers, has led writing groups and workshops in OK, KS and CO. She is the author of <u>Rain Forest Girl</u>, and is working on a mainstream novel, <u>The House on Cherry Street</u>, and <u>Long River Home</u>, a historical novel.

Sharon Newman is author of 14 books on quilt making, a teacher, and appraiser. For 21 years she owned The Quilt Shop in Lubbock, TX. She is known for her knowledge of quilt patterns and history, and has a collection of quilts spanning 200 years.

Virginia Newton, Virginia Newton completed her BA at Western NMU and her counseling degree at Northern AZU. She and Paul have one daughter, Christy. After careers in education and counseling, they retired to their Texas farm where she quilts.

Dan R. Olsen received his BS degree in Electrical Engineering from Oklahoma State University in 1986. Dan is currently an Engineer with Bluebonnet Electric in Giddings, TX. Dan's Children's Story, *The Mysterious Ring,* won 1st Place in 2003.

Sara Orwig is the author of 71 published novels with over 20 million copies in print in 23 languages with over 230 foreign translations.

Muriel Pech Owen of Cedar Rapids, IO, is the founding President of East Iowa Heirloom Quilters. She delights in sharing both her quilts and her stories, stating she finds quilters to be the best of kind people with warm and open hearts.

Irene Ruth Rennhack is a long-time quilter in Oceanside, CA. She's been a member of the Santa Clara Valley Quilt Association, **Director of the American Museum of Quilts**, and currently a member of the El Camino Quilt Guild.

Martha Rhynes is a nonfiction writer since her retirement as an English teacher. She lives with her husband on a family owned and operated commercial cattle ranch in South Central OK and has six adult children and 12 grandchildren.

T. Dawn Richard, the mother of four children lives in Spokane, WA. She writes mysteries and enjoys racquetball. Her husband, Glenn has flown for the Air Force for 21 years and is looking forward to retirement and a new career.

Rhonda Richards graduated Phi Beta Kappa from Birmingham-Southern College with a double major in English and history. An avid quilter, she has edited more than a dozen quilting publications and now works as a copy editor for a national magazine.

Delores Ann Patton Rieck, 1938, graduated from Emporia State University in KS and entered the teaching profession. Marriage and two children followed. According to her mother, a piece of fabric was her favorite toy

Barbara Shepherd has won more than 100 writing awards in regional and international literary contests, with 50% placing in the top three, for fiction, non-fiction, poetry and screenplay. Her creative and technical work appears in books, magazines and newspapers.

M. Carolyn Steele retired from a commercial art career to pursue a love of writing and has completed two award-winning novels. Combining her knowledge of storytelling and genealogy, she presents programs to inspire others to preserve their family legends.

Lynda Stephenson is a retired English professor from East Central University who reads, travels, and collects art. She lives in Edmond, OK with her husband and two cats. <u>Dancing with Elvis</u>, her first novel, will be available in the fall of 2005.

Jean Stover is a retired Business teacher who keeps busy at writing, drama, choirs, and painting.

Beverly Tucker Vokoun was married to Bobby Tucker for 12 years before he was killed in a motorcycle accident in 1977. They had four girls and one boy. Beverly is self- employed and currently married to Jim Vokoun for 20 years.

Teresa C. Vratil grew up on a farm in KS with six brothers and sisters. Her mother was a city girl transplanted to the farm. She grew up with the dual expectation of working outdoors, but doing it in a ladylike manner.

Kelly Weir and her husband Russ have twin 20-year-old daughters. She is a board member of Arise Ministries and the Prayer Ministry Coordinator for Arise and for her church Women's Ministry.

Pam Whitley, a native of MI, married Mike Whitley in 1970 and became a bonifide "Okie!" with two children and two grandchildren. Pam's love for quilts began as a child watching her grandmas piece quilt tops. Pam is a freelance writer and speaker.

Regina Yoder believes her three children and six grandchildren are each created in a special pattern — projects that God is still completing. She learned to quilt from her strict Amish mother-in-law, whose goal was 12 stitches to the inch.

Dorothy Palmer Young is a seamstress, desktop publisher, and freelance writer. Her work appears in several anthologies. She and her husband Bob make their home in Edmond, OK. She has recently started quilting.

Who is Judy Howard?

Since 1976, Judy Howard has owned and operated Buckboard Antiques and Quilts in Oklahoma City, Oklahoma.

Her love of quilts developed while taking a class from nationally renowned fiber artist Terrie Mangat. Judy became a charter member of the Oklahoma Quilt Guild, and antique quilts became her specialty.

Julia Roberts, America's sweetheart, likes to give Wedding Ring quilts when her family and friends marry. Jessica Lange and Dustin Hoffman are also celebrity clients, Dustin purchasing 17 quilts while he was in town filming Rainman.

Judy recently moved her shop home to concentrate on her web business and to write for God's glory. Her mail order business offers photos of 250 antique quilts, tops, and blocks. You can visit Judy's Website at www.buckboardquilts.com to view her online inventory of quality quilts at affordable prices.

Rhonda Richards, Editor, recently honored Judy by featuring Buckboard Quilts in their book, **Great American Quilts 2004**. Many of Judy's articles and quilts are showcased in quilt magazines and books.

After graduating in 1966 with honors from Oklahoma Baptist University and doing graduate work at Oklahoma State University, Judy and her husband, Bill, purchased and operated Howard Equipment Company for ten years. Then, quilting won her heart!

Heavenly Patchwork was awarded the Golden Seal as an Oklahoma Centennial Project. One story will appear in **Chicken Soup for the Christian Soul II**. OKC Metro Library placed **Heavenly Patchwork** in its Oklahoma Room. Stories won Second and Third Place in the regional OWFI Writing Contest.

Judy now presents *"Historic Quilts of America,"* a power point program which includes a writing workshop, 250 quilts from museums, Buckboard's collection and **Heavenly Patchwork**. She exhibits "911" and Murrah Memorial Quilts at quilt shows, guilds, book signings, libraries, women's clubs, schools, art galleries, museums and churches and others. To schedule a program, book signing, exhibit, see/purchase her quilts or submit stories call 405-751-3885 or email at *BuckboardQuilts@cox.net.*

ORDER HERE

_____ Yes, I want _____ copies of Heavenly Patchwork for $12.95 each.

Include $2.50 shipping and handling for one book, and $1.50 for each additional book. Oklahoma residents must include applicable sales tax of $1.08 per book. Canadian orders must include payment in US funds, with 7% GST added. Supplies are limited, so order today.

Payment must accompany orders. Allow 2 weeks for delivery.

For an excellent Fund-Raiser, I will donate to your nonprofit Quilt Guild, Church or group $7 for each book when you buy 32 – $7.50 each on a 64 book order – $8 each on a 96 book order. Add $13/box of 32 books for actual media mail shipping cost.

Order 32 books for $5.95 each + $13 shipping = $203.40
Order 64 books for $5.45 each + $26 shipping = $374.80
Order 96 books for $4.95 each + $39 shipping = $514.20

My check or money order for $ _____ for _____ books is enclosed

Name _____

Organization _____

Address _____

City/State/Zip _____

Phone _____ Email _____

For questions call 405-751-3885
Make your check payable and return to
Dorcas Publishing
12101 N. MacArthur, Suite 137
Oklahoma City, OK 73162-1800
www.heavenlypatchwork.com